Indian Saddle-Up

INDIAN SADDLE-UP

Glenn Balch

Illustrated by Robert Frankenberg

THOMAS Y. CROWELL COMPANY

NEW YORK

To my son Olin
May he know and enjoy the same fine pleasures of horses and the outdoors which have so enriched my own life

Indian Saddle-Up

CHAPTER ONE

TWO INDIANS were walking across the rolling grassy prairie. They were young, slim, and wiry and wore only breechcloths and moccasins. Their moccasins were low cut, with long fringes dragging from the heels to blur and obscure the young men's footprints. The dragging fringes showed them to be of the wandering tribes which the white men would come to know as the Comanches. Their hair was straight and dark and it fell, long and loose, over their shoulders. Their eyes were dark too, and their skin was a deep reddish brown. They carried bows of dark wood hanging beside painted rawhide quivers of arrows on their backs. At the brow of each rise they would pause to scan carefully the country beyond.

This was the plains country—the Staked Plains, as the area would be called a hundred years later when it became part of the Texas Panhandle. There were long successive sweeps of rolling grass lands, with occasional clumps of runs of low, heavily leafed trees. Here and there in the deeper valleys were the watercourses, marked by brush and trees of a lighter green. Many of these were now dry and the water stood almost motionless and turgid in the others. The grass was brittle and brown, and the brassy noonday sun caused shimmering heat waves to rise from the land. It was the year 1715, and white men across the sea had barely heard of the great grasslands that lay at the heart of the continent.

The first youth walked with an effortless, swinging stride, light in the tufted grass and sure, but not so the second. His gait had a peculiar hitch in it, a thump and a jar. And one of his moccasins, the right, had an unusual shape, almost round. But the leg above that deformed foot was strong and well-shaped and this youth kept close behind the other. Too, he carried his bow and arrow as readily.

At the next crest, after stealthily rising to peer over, they sank back quickly to the grass. A small band of great hump-shouldered beasts was feeding in the little valley. They were buffalo.

The first youth lifted himself for a second look. "If our father were here, that young bull feeding this side of the herd would be his," he said.

The youth with the lame foot nodded and lifted his own head to look. "The first the bull would know would be when the arrow struck his heart," he said. "Our father is so skillful he could get very close, even though there is almost no cover."

Follows Bees, the first youth, watched the grazing animals thoughtfully. "I have not yet killed a buffalo," he

[2]

said. "I would like to kill one. The meat and skin would be welcome in our lodge."

"Yes," Twisted Foot said. He had not killed a buffalo either, but he did not make a point of it, for he knew no one expected him to, not with his unsightly crippled foot. Nevertheless, he would have much liked to. Buffalo meat was always hailed with great delight in his father's lodge and the hides, with their thick shaggy fur, were prized possessions of many uses. It was a fortunate day for the Indian who secured one of the big animals, for they were not only fleet of foot but possessed a remarkably keen sense of smell to warn them of danger. Indeed, many of the buffalo that fell to the Comanches in those days were the old and weak or those which in some manner had become crippled and unable to flee.

Twisted Foot raised his head and looked again, hopefully, then shook his head. All of these buffalo seemed to be in excellent health, entirely capable of running away from even Follows Bees, who was well known to be the fleetest runner in their band. Follows Bees could run at a good pace for half a day, but the buffalo would leave him far behind.

"I will try to get close to the bull," Follows Bees whispered presently. "They are not yet warned. This is an opportunity too rare to miss."

Twisted Foot nodded. "I could try for that smaller one, over there," he said. "Perhaps I could get it."

[3]

"No," Follows Bees said. "You will scare them. They will hear your clumsy foot. I will go alone."

"Very well," Twisted Foot agreed. It was always this way—he could not do things as well as his brother. If a buffalo was killed, it would of course be Follows Bees that killed it. Follows Bees did everything well and would one day be a great hunter. "I will wait here," he said. "But get close. And make sure of your aim. Remember, the big humps have tough skins."

The two youths had of course been hunting into the wind, for otherwise the buffalo would already have smelled them. But on that hot sultry day very little wind was moving. This was not good for it meant that their scent hung in the air about them like invisible dust and a vagrant drift might easily carry it to the animals. But it could not be helped.

Follows Bees raised his lean body as high as he dared and studied the slope and the cover for several minutes. It was short grass, close growing, with scattered taller bushes and a few straggling weeds. Twisted Foot knew a man might hide in such grass by lying very still, like an antelope fawn, but it was not tall enough to cover movement. Their father, One Grass, might be able to do it, for he was the band's cleverest stalker and had killed several buffalo. His very name was a tribute to his ability to remain unseen in a minimum of cover. Follows Bees was anxious to prove himself in this important Indian skill also, and he studied the ground carefully, the shallow depressions, the almost unseen rises.

[4]

After a time Follows Bees pushed back from the crest until he could sit upright without danger of being seen by the buffalo. He sprinkled dust on his already dark legs and arms and chest, and Twisted Foot threw still more dust on his back, hiding the shine which the sun made on the skin. Twisted Foot sprinkled dust until his brother's straight black hair was grey. Follows Bees took off his quiver and selected from it his heaviest and straightest arrow. He inspected the feathers and made certain that the chipped stone head was tight in its fastenings of twisted sinew.

Satisfied with his preparations, Follows Bees gave his quiver to Twisted Foot for safekeeping, turned on his stomach and wriggled away along the crest of the rise, gripping both the bow and the heavy arrow in his left hand. Twisted Foot watched him go, already knowing the roundabout route Follows Bees would take. If the buffalo continued feeding in their present direction and did not become alarmed, Follows Bees might be close enough to the separately-grazing bull for a shot in an hour's time. Follows Bees was careful and patient and would drive his arrow hard and true.

Twisted Foot remained where he was, a still dark figure in the dry grass. His eyes were slitted against the bright glare of the sun and he might easily have been asleep. But he wasn't. His keenly-developed senses of hearing and smell were alert, and periodically his eyes widened for a glance at the sun-washed plain.

There was a movement on a rise half a mile away.

[5]

Twisted Foot made no perceptible movement but he knew immediately that it was an antelope, a cautious male peering over the crest. Even at that distance he could make out the high black horns, curving inwardly at the tips. Antelope were the game which he and Follows Bees had been most hopeful of securing and he watched the buck with interest. Antelope could see much better than buffalo and were fleeter, being able to run around startled buffalo, a trick they sometimes used for protection. One might think that they would be more difficult for the Indians to secure, and they would have been, had it not been for an ingrained curiosity which impelled them to investigate anything they did not understand.

Twisted Foot had a piece of soft white buckskin, attached to a long slender stick like a flag. This was what he and Follows Bees used to attract the attention of antelope, and now he considered raising it, knowing that there would be other animals behind the buck. After a second's thought, however, he decided against this, unwilling to do anything that might startle the grazing buffalo. Often the antelope would run in circles about a flag before approaching it, and their agitation might give warning to the larger beasts, making Follows Bees' stalk useless.

It turned out to be a large band of antelope, males and females, old and young. Their dark horns and the white bars across their necks glistened in the sun as they came stepping daintily on slender legs over the crest. They

[6]

grazed with lowered heads but always, no matter how good the grass, there were several heads raised and alert. They grazed through the swale at an angle and Twisted Foot watched them, thinking that if Follows Bees were not successful in stalking the buffalo they might, later, try for an antelope.

A short time afterward, and far beyond the feeding antelope, another animal came into Twisted Foot's view. It was too far for him to see clearly through the heat haze and he wondered idly what it might be. It looked too big for an antelope and was probably a plains deer. He watched it, thinking that it might come his way. He would like to have a deer, for the meat was excellent and the skins had many uses, but they were more easily killed in the ravine country than on the plains. Through the haze the animal took queer shapes and presently one reminded him of the strange creatures that Old Man Crazy told about so often.

Old Man Crazy was a strange person himself. He was the oldest Indian in Kills Something's band, a dried leathery old man with only one eye and bent, gnarled hands. He was a Comanche, as was proved by his familiarity with the language, but he had traveled in far places and years before had come from the south and attached himself to the village. Often there were strange gleams in his one good eye and there were long cruel scars on his old bent back. He was usually moody and silent but sometimes angry and talkative, and when he was talkative he

[7]

told strange and impossible tales, tales of men whose skin was white and whose hair was not always black but often yellow, like the color of cottonwood leaves in the fall. The Comanches allowed all their old men to do as they pleased, but Old Man Crazy really acted *strange*. He told stories of men who wore hard bright shells about their bodies, shells brighter and stronger than even those of the armadillo, shells that arrowheads made a noise against but did not go through. He told of bright sharp knives and hatchets that would split a skull without crushing the bone, and of magic smoke-sticks that could bring death to a man or animal farther than an arrow's flight away. He told of many things, so strange and fantastic they could not be believed, and Kills Something and the men of the village, while listening, would shake their heads, sending the old man into angry protests that what he told about was true.

Twisted Foot had listened with the others and with even greater interest, for the stories stirred his keen imagination and he was impressed by Old Man Crazy's obvious sincerity, though not even he could believe all the impossible things. But he liked to listen most when Old Man Crazy told about the strange animals, the animals that had been with the men with the white skins. As Old Man Crazy told it, these animals were amazingly big, and possessed great strength and ferocity. They did all kinds of unbelievable things, even following the men with the white skins and sometimes actually carrying the men on

[8]

their backs. That is what Old Man Crazy had said, that and a lot more. He had even described the animals, telling how they had long necks and big heads, how the hair grew long and thick at the top of their necks, and how their tails were also long and thick and sometimes swept the very grass itself. Twisted Foot shook his head, knowing that it could not be true. Kills Something and all the men knew it could not be true. It was just a strange wild dream that had become fixed in Old Man Crazy's somewhat bewildered head. There were no such animals of course, nor any men with white skins. But if there were, well, he would like to see them. It would be very helpful to have an animal carry him on its back, because of his crippled foot. He never told anyone but sometimes, after listening to Old Man Crazy, he had strange and impossible dreams himself, dreams of moving swiftly across the prairie, as easily and smoothly as a bird on wing. They were like the dreams of guardian spirits he had heard the old men describe.

Twisted Foot pushed these thoughts from his mind and found that the distant animal had now disappeared. He was certain it had been a deer, but he would like to know for sure. Perhaps, going back to the village, he and Follows Bees could go that way.

Now he knew that Follows Bees was over the crest, that with his good feet he was pushing himself slowly and carefully through the grass, using the cover of each of the small bushes, never raising his head, yet watching constantly, pulling his bow and arrow along at his side. It would be necessary to get close, for an arrow must be driven deep between the ribs. But Follows Bees knew that as well as he.

A gust of wind rippled the dry grass. Twisted Foot took quick notice of it, since he knew immediately that it could spoil Follows Bees' plans. By now, Follows Bees should be around the low nose and well to the front of the grazing herd, where both its movements and his own would serve to narrow the distance. Given time, the bull should feed within yards of him. But this wind—it would carry Follows Bees' scent across the prairie. One whiff and the buffalo would whirl and flee, most likely in the opposite direction.

A quick idea came to Twisted Foot. He turned over on his stomach and wriggled through the grass, dragging his own bow and Follows Bees' quiver. At the top of the crest he saw the buffalo. They were farther away now, having been feeding steadily, but he noted with satisfaction that they had not changed their course. He did not waste time trying to see Follows Bees but wriggled on as rapidly as he could push himself with his good foot. The other one was not much good for that purpose, but he had learned that long ago.

Twisted Foot slithered on. He took a course which would eventually put him to the windward of the buffalo herd and this, for a hunter, seemed foolish. But Twisted Foot had an idea. Behind a clump of brush he scampered forward on his hands and knees. He went on. Now the wind was blowing steadily. Twisted Foot cut directly across it, making no effort to get nearer the buffalo. He heard the snort, however, when presently an old bull caught his scent, and he watched as the animal whirled in his direction and stared with beady black eyes almost lost in the heavy matted hair that covered its broad skull.

An instant later the bull whirled back, bellowing. Then the herd was running. Twisted Foot sat up, watching and hoping that his calculations had been correct. If not, he would hear unpleasantly from Follows Bees for having spoiled the stalk.

A young bull running at the side stumbled and went down, with a thump and a grunt that Twisted Foot could plainly hear. Twisted Foot leaped to his feet and ran as fast as he could. Follows Bees appeared from the grass. The young bull regained its feet and charged on after the others, but it ran unsteadily and with heavy pounding. It fell again, got up and moved on. The distance between it and the others widened, and soon it stopped and stood, its great head lowered. Twisted Foot and Follows Bees came up to it. Its eyes were glazed and blood sprayed from its dark nostrils at each discharge of breath.

Follows Bees took his quiver from Twisted Foot, put an arrow in his bow, went in close and drove the arrow deep into the great brown side. The buffalo gave no notice of this new hurt, but soon began to sway on his short front legs. A minute later it toppled over. Follows Bees drew

[11]

his stone knife, approached from the back and sawed through the tough hide and into the jugular vein. "It is a fine buffalo," he said proudly. "Our father will be pleased."

"Our mother will be happy with the skin also," Twisted Foot said. "Your arrow went to the right place."

"Yes," Follows Bees agreed, trying to be modest. "I will kill many buffalo. We will feast on the liver. I am hungry." He began to cut into the animal's belly.

Twisted Foot took out his own knife and helped his brother. As he worked, he marveled at what a big fine animal it was, fat and strong. Few such fell to the Indians. Follows Bees had good reason to be proud, for this would earn him recognition in the village.

They secured the liver from the cavity and pulled it out hot and dripping. With their knives they cut off slivers and ate them. It had been long hours since they had eaten and they were hungry, and they considered fresh raw liver one of the best of foods. Too, many long hours of walking and carrying faced them before they could reach the village that night.

"We will return tomorrow and get some more meat," Follows Bees said.

"If the wolves leave any," Twisted Foot said. "We will take the hide with us, to make certain they do not spoil that." He cut another slice of liver, which all this time had been dwindling with amazing rapidity.

"Perhaps our mother and Rabbit Woman will come

with us tomorrow," Follows Bees said happily. "And we will bring dogs. We will come early and carry back all that remains. Our father's lodge will have much meat, brother."

Twisted Foot nodded. "The dogs will help us carry it, and also they will help us eat it, for they like buffalo meat as well as their cousins, the grey wolves. We must tie it to the travois so they cannot reach it with their mouths."

"We will," Follows Bees said. "They may have some small pieces for helping us. Without them, we would have to carry everything on our backs."

"Yes," Twisted Foot answered. "It would be helpful," he went on, "if we had one of those big animals about which Old Man Crazy talks. It would carry the buffalo."

"A horse?" Follows Bees said, scoffing. "There is no such animal, brother. You know it as well as I. It is one of the things Old Man Crazy sees with his blind eye."

"Yes, but it would be helpful," Twisted Foot insisted.

"It would be helpful also if this were a white buffalo and would bring us the favor of the spirits," Follows Bees said, "but it is not. We should be thankful, brother, that we have good buffalo meat to carry. Now let us take the hide. Night will come before we are back at the village." He began cutting at the tough hide with his stone knife.

Ingrained habit caused Twisted Foot to take a look around before he knelt to help with the task. "Look, brother!" he cried with sudden concern. "Who is that?"

Some distance away a number of men were coming

[13]

across the prairie in a compact group. They were Indians, dark of hair and skin, and dressed in shorter breechcloths than those worn by Twisted Foot and his brother.

"Down!" Follows Bees cried quickly. "We must hide."

"It is too late," Twisted Foot said. "Already they have seen me."

Follows Bees gave an unhappy cry. "They are our enemies, the Utes," he said.

"Yes," Twisted Foot agreed. "They carry war spears, as well as bows and arrows. There are no women or children with them."

"They will take our buffalo," Follows Bees said dismally. "They will take the robe and the meat."

Twisted Foot was thinking of something still more serious. "They come searching for our village," he said. "They know that they are many and we are few. They come to fight us again, brother." He shook his head sorrowfully at the thought.

The men had now altered their direction and were coming straight toward the two youths. Those in front increased their pace to a trot with obvious eagerness.

Follows Bees, who all this time had been kneeling, snatched an arrow from his quiver and fitted it to his bow.

"No," Twisted Foot said firmly. "We must flee, brother."

"And leave our buffalo?" Follows Bees cried bitterly.

"Yes," Twisted Foot said. "Our chief must be warned as soon as possible. It will be necessary to move the village back to the big ravines, to a place where the Utes dare not come. In a battle our father might be killed, and our other brothers, and the women and girls would be taken as slaves."

"How?" Follows Bees asked bewilderedly. "If we run to the village, the Utes will be at our heels. There will be no time for hiding."

Twisted Foot had already thought of this. "As yet they have seen only me; they do not know you are here. Crawl away through the grass, as when you were stalking the buffalo. Go at once to the village and tell Chief Kills Something. I will delay the Utes."

"But they will catch you," Follows Bees said. "You cannot run fast to get away from them. I can run much faster."

"That is why *you* must go to our village," Twisted Foot said. "Hurry, brother. Start at once."

Follows Bees hesitated another second, then fell full length to the grass and began wriggling away. Twisted Foot leaped over the carcass of the buffalo and began to run to the south. With cries and shouts, brandishing their weapons, the Utes swung their course to intercept him, encouraged by the fact that he ran with shortened stride.

The Comanche village was in a grove of tall willows and cottonwoods beside a stream to the east.

CHAPTER TWO

THE TWISTED FOOT was the result of an accident which had occurred when the Comanche youth was very small. He had fallen on sharp rocks and the muscles and tendons of his inner foot had been severely slashed. The healing had shortened them, pulling the toes and fore part of his foot inward until he walked mostly on the curved outer edge. The joints had fused together, destroying normal flexibility, and when the boy walked again, it was with a shortened limping stride. And inevitably, after the manner of the Comanches, he soon became known as Little Twisted Foot.

He was, however, an active, interested lad and did not permit his deformity to set him apart from the others. On the contrary, he entered into the activities and games of Indian boyhood with even more zeal and enthusiasm. He proved that he could walk and swim, and shoot a bow, even that he could run, though in the races he was soon outdistanced. Among a people who put much store on fleetness of foot, this was of course disappointing, but the boy did not complain. Instead, he sought to make up for his frailty by becoming more skillful in other activities, such as shooting, stalking, sign-reading and knowledge of the many animals, large and small, about which Indian life revolved.

Now, however, with the Utes at his heels, speed in running became the all-important thing. Twisted Foot tried, pounding along on his crippled foot as rapidly as he could, but soon the Utes were close behind him. There were no flying arrows and he knew the reason; they wanted him as a captive. He ran his best but a powerful brown arm came around his neck and jerked him roughly to the ground. The Utes immediately surrounded him, several threatening him with half-raised lances. They were square, solid men, and their expressions were stern and hostile.

"Why does my brother flee?" one, evidently the leader, asked in broken Comanche.

"Why do the Utes seek to harm me?" Twisted Foot countered bluntly.

The man glared at him. "You are an evening from the ravine country," he said. "You are a Comanche."

Twisted Foot did not answer, knowing there would be no point in denying it. Besides, he was proud of being a Comanche. The Comanches, he was certain, were the strongest and bravest people in the world, and when they were equal in numbers to the Utes, they would not run.

"Are you of the village of Chief Kills Something?" the Ute leader asked, with a show of friendliness.

[17]

Without seeming to look, Twisted Foot noted that there were many of them, and that in addition to their bows and lances they carried stone-headed axes. There could be no question but that they had come to fight, to kill, and to secure captives.

"Where is Kills Something's village?" the leader asked.

Twisted Foot thought of Follows Bees and hoped that his brother had gotten away safely.

"Where is your village?" the leader asked again, angrily.

"Over there," Twisted Foot said, pointing to the south.

The leader's eyelids lowered shrewdly, and one of the other men said, "He lies. The village is there." He pointed to the east. "I saw it myself." ·

Twisted Foot's expression did not change. That the Utes knew where the village lay was no surprise to him. He had surmised as much when he saw the size of the party. A hunter or a scout, probably the man who had spoken, had seen the village and carried the news back to his chief.

"Kills Something is in Ute country," the leader told Twisted Foot accusingly.

"He is not," Twisted Foot retorted with spirit. "The Utes are in Comanche country. These are the plains of our fathers."

The leader shrugged and said, "That is not true. These are Ute hunting grounds. We will drive the Comanche dogs out. Bind his arms."

[18]

Two of the warriors seized Twisted Foot from behind. They took his bow and arrows and his knife and tied his wrists behind his back with a buckskin thong.

"Come on," the leader said, and turned to the east.

Twisted Foot thought rapidly. "The buffalo will go to the wolves," he said. "They will ruin the fine hide."

The leader halted. A buffalo was as much a prize to the Utes as to the Comanches. "What buffalo?" he demanded.

"The one I killed," Twisted Foot said. "It is a fine fat one."

"Where is it?" the leader asked.

"Back there," Twisted Foot said. "Have the Utes no eyes, that they did not see it?" In his mind he thought: by now, Follows Bees is running swiftly through the big swale.

The leader looked at his men questioningly. They shook their heads. "Take us to this buffalo," he directed Twisted Foot.

Twisted Foot shrugged and said, "The wolves are welcome to it."

The man struck him sharply with a lance shaft and said, "Show us where it is."

Twisted Foot said, "I will show you if you will give me what I can eat of the hump."

"Very well," the leader said. "Take us to it."

Twisted Foot turned and went back across the prairie. The Utes followed him, watchful and somewhat impatient. Twisted Foot kept walking.

"Where is it?" the leader demanded presently. "We have already wasted too much time."

"It is here—some place," Twisted Foot said, looking about in a puzzled manner.

"Find it quickly," the leader ordered.

Twisted Foot walked some more, turning this way and that. But still he couldn't find the buffalo.

"Enough of this," the Ute leader said presently. "I do not believe you have killed a buffalo." He glanced down at the young Comanche's injured foot.

"Yes I did," Twisted Foot said stoutly.

"Then we will leave it," the leader said.

"Now I remember," Twisted Foot said. "It is over this way." He turned and led the way over the grass.

"We will wait no longer," the Ute leader said, after following a few minutes.

"There it is," Twisted Foot said, pointing.

The dark body was visible in the grass. Immediately the Utes ran to it and began examining it. "It is a fine buffalo," the leader said. He looked into the cavity. "Where is the liver?"

"I ate it," Twisted Foot said. Then, noticing the doubt in the leader's eyes, he added, "What I could not eat, I threw away. Here are chips for a fire." He turned up a piece of dried dung with the toe of his moccasin. By now, Follows Bees should be ascending the broad crest, the one with the lone tree on it.

"There is not time for a fire," the Ute leader said. "We will carry the meat with us. Tonight we will feast."

He has plans, Twisted Foot thought. He is in a hurry.

"Thank you, Comanche, for showing us a fine buffalo," the leader said. "But how could you, with a crippled foot, kill it?"

"It is not with my feet that I draw a bow," Twisted Foot replied. By now, Follows Bees should be on the crest and he would not pause, but would regain his breath on the downward side.

"Skin it quickly and cut up the meat," the Ute leader directed.

With the pieces of sharpened stone they used for knives, the Utes skinned the buffalo and cut the meat into chunks convenient for carrying. Scraps and choice bits were eaten as they worked. In a short time they were again on their way, moving eastward after the stern leader. Twisted Foot was in the rear, with two men assigned to guard him. He lagged, exaggerating his limp and seeking to delay the march, but one of the men prodded him sharply with the fire-hardened point of a lance.

They traveled steadily through the afternoon, a strong body of men with fleet scouts to the front and sides. The leader was constantly alert, giving orders and watching the scouts for signals. Twisted Foot was dismayed by the trueness of their course: it was evident that there were those among them who knew exactly where the Comanche village lay. By now, Follows Bees should be at the first creek. There was a crossing where he could wade without wetting more than his moccasins, but he would take the shorter way and swim the deep pool, holding his bow and quiver above the water.

One thing encouraged Twisted Foot and this was the approaching darkness. Already it was late in the afternoon. When night came to the prairie, it would come swiftly.

They crossed the first stream at the ford at dusk. The Utes drank and permitted Twisted Foot to throw himself down too. They went on into the fringe of brush and trees. Twisted Foot had hoped that a halt might be made there, where wood was to be had for the cooking fires, but the leader did not pause. Now Follows Bees would be at the second and smaller creek, where those who knew could cross quickly over a fallen tree.

Twisted Foot could hear the soft noise of the moccasins in the dry grass about him. The stars were bright in the high dome of the sky. The Utes were dark silent forms, striding steadily. One of the guards put a loop of leather about Twisted Foot's neck and walked in front with the end of the loop tied to his belt. The second one followed behind with ready lance. There was no talking, no sound save the rustle of moccasins and the whisper of the night wind.

On and on they went, holding a course for the Comanche village as true as Twisted Foot himself would have followed, making it apparent that the raid had been carefully planned. The young Comanche was dismayed by the knowledge and fretted against his helplessness. Kills Something's village might be destroyed, and his mother and father and sisters and brothers along with it. Yet he could do nothing.

On the Utes went. The hours of the night passed to the steady rustle of feet in the grass. Twisted Foot's deep concern was occasionally interrupted by a stinging prod from behind, warning him to keep up.

They arrived at the second creek and here, under cover of the leafy trees, the leader halted. The men immediately scattered, collecting wood for their fires. Twisted Foot could hear the limbs and twigs breaking in the dark. His guards made sure of him by quickly tying his ankles to the trunk of a small tree. They tied his wrists behind his back. He could sit or lie down, but had no chance to free himself.

Their leader had promised them a feast and they had it, eating buffalo meat boiled in the stomach of the animal. Twisted Foot watched them resentfully, feeling that this meat rightfully belonged to his own people. He was hungry too, but no one came to keep the leader's promise that he should have part of the choice hump meat. He was not surprised and he determined that he would not beg. They should see a Comanche's pride.

As the Utes finished eating, they lay down around the fires and Twisted Foot knew they planned to stay here for some time. He tried his wrist bonds again, hoping that in some way he might loosen them. One of the guards came to look at him, tested the knots and, finding them tight, gave Twisted Foot a push with his foot that sent the youth full length to the ground. Twisted Foot lay there indifferently and the man soon went back to the others.

Now Follows Bees should be at the village. Now he should have told Kills Something that the Utes were coming. Now the Comanches should be gathering their possessions and packing the dogs. Still Twisted Foot could not help but worry. What if something had gone wrong, if Follows Bees had not arrived to warn them? Twisted Foot tried hard to break the leg bonds that held him to the tree, but he could not.

After some time the leader went about, kicking the sleeping men awake. It was still dark, still a long time before day would come, and Twisted Foot knew then that the plan was to arrive at the village just before dawn. The attack would be made in the first light, when the Utes could see and before the unsuspecting Comanches were fully awake. The Utes would have the advantage of surprise as well as superior numbers. Twisted Foot prayed to his guardian spirit that the plan would not succeed.

One of the guards came and untied Twisted Foot. Another jerked him to his feet and prodded him into action with a lance. They waded the stream and moved in the darkness across the prairie, a grim, silent group.

Twisted Foot knew they were still half a mile from the

village when the leader halted and voiced a curt command. Instantly several of the men seized the young Comanche. They threw him to the ground and tied him firmly, hand and foot, with strong straps. Then they left him there, moved on, and were soon lost in the night.

Twisted Foot made an attempt to get to his feet, but could not. Indeed, the only parts of his body that he could move were his fingers and toes. He was helpless—and the Utes had gone to attack his people. He turned and jerked in desperate effort, hoping to find some weakness in his bonds. But there was none. Presently he gave up.

Time passed slowly after that for the young Comanche. He wished he could hold back the dawn, that on this day the great fiery Sun god would not come. But presently light appeared in the east, at first low and faint along the rim of the prairie. Then, bit by bit, it flared upward, turning the sky to silver. In his mind, Twisted Foot could see the Utes, ferocious and determined, charging the brush wickiups of the village. He could see the men— Kills Something, his father and the others—rushing to the doorways to be met by flights of deadly arrows. He hid his face in the grass and prayed to his Spirit Guardian.

Twisted Foot had many torturing misgivings before the Utes returned. He heard them coming and lifted his head. There were only four of them, with a tall lean man in front. Twisted Foot studied his face, searching for information. The face was dark and stern, telling him nothing.

"What occurred?" Twisted Foot asked, unable to restrain his impatience. "Where are the others?"

The man did not reply. He knelt, untied the leg bonds and hauled Twisted Foot to his feet. Twisted Foot found that he could hardly stand. "Did you find the village?" he cried. "Where are the others? Was there a battle?"

"The Comanche dogs will not escape," the tall man said angrily. "You," he went on, "will be my slave. I will take you back to our village and you will have to work with the women."

"They did escape," Twisted Foot said happily. "You did not find them. They were gone."

"My leader and his men will find them," the Ute retorted. "Even now they are following the trail. The Comanches run like women."

"It is wise to run when you are few," Twisted Foot told him. "But one day they will be many."

"The Utes will catch them," the man said. "They will never come back to the plains."

"That is only a Ute hope," an irritated old voice said. "The time will come when the Comanches will rule the plains."

Twisted Foot whirled and saw the old man, his one good eye glittering with wrathful indignation. "Old Man Crazy!" he cried in surprise. "How is it you are here? Did you not have time to flee?" In his consternation he had not noticed the old Comanche among them.

[27]

"Yes, there was time," Old Man Crazy said. "But I had not finished my sleep."

"The Utes caught you?" Twisted Foot cried, knowing, of course, that they had.

"Women, women," Old Man Crazy said scornfully of his captors. "They catch none but children and old men."

Being called a "woman" is an insult to an Indian man, and the tall Ute was angered so strongly that he stepped toward Old Man Crazy and drew back his lance.

"Wait!" Twisted Foot cried in sharp warning. "Do not strike. He is a strange one."

"A strange one?" the Ute said, lowering his arm, for among the Indians there was a supernatural fear of harming persons whose minds were strange or queer. It was believed that such people were under the special protection of the spirits.

"Yes," Twisted Foot said. "His head is puzzled. He often tells of strange and impossible things. It would bring bad luck if he should be hurt."

The Ute hesitated, not knowing whether to believe Twisted Foot or not. He looked closely at Old Man Crazy, at the old man's lean leathery face and at his single glittering eye.

"I have seen the men with the white skins," Old Man Crazy said. "They carry thunder and lightning in their hands."

The Ute looked at Twisted Foot and asked, "Of what does he speak?"

[28]

Twisted Foot shrugged and said, "Who knows? It is often that he is like that."

The Ute looked at his two fellow tribesmen. Their faces were worried and puzzled. "Come," the tall one said. "We will take these two to our village and see how it pleases them to do the work of women. When our leader returns, we can decide whether to kill them."

CHAPTER THREE

CLAIMING A large part of the buffalo range, the Utes were the enemies not only of the Comanches but also of any others who sought to move into the territory. Many in numbers and wide-ranging, they zealously guarded what they insisted were their hereditary rights, making savage forays against any who dared dispute them. And they had proved themselves to be bold and relentless warriors.

Kills Something was well aware of this, for in the past his village had suffered humiliating defeats at the hands of the Utes, but the big buffalo herds with their wealth of meat and skins had been a temptation that the Comanches could not resist. The hides were particularly desirable, since from them the Indians could make excellent clothes and bedding. The Comanches, as were all the Great Plains Indians, were sometimes a wandering people, on the move in search of game. So Kills Something and his men had decided to risk the wrath of the Utes in an effort to secure buffalo skins.

Now Twisted Foot, moving across the prairie with his

hands tied behind his back and guarded by three Ute warriors, knew the venture had turned out badly. They had been discovered before they had time to do much hunting. He and Old Man Crazy were captives, and the village was fleeing from the Ute war party. Instead of securing the hides they had hoped for, the Comanches were running for their lives.

Twisted Foot knew Kills Something had made a wise decision. To stay and fight against the superior number of the Utes would have been stupid. Nevertheless, Twisted Foot was worried and humiliated. He was worried because he was not certain the village would escape, and humiliated because his people had been forced to flee. There had been a time, he had been told, when the proud Comanches had run from no people. That time, he told himself determinedly, would come again. The time would come when they would hunt where and when they wished, without fear or favor, when they would stride boldly and openly across the plains and be wealthy in buffalo hides and meat. But now the Utes were too many.

The little group moved steadily across the wide rolling plains, moccasined feet raising a mustiness from the dry dusty grass. The bright sun drilled the lean coppery bodies with its heat and the glint of perspiration appeared on shoulders and arms. The tall Ute moved in front, and the two others came behind, their lances ready. Occasionally Twisted Foot could hear Old Man Crazy mumbling to himself indignantly at the discomfort and inconvenience of the travel. "Are the Utes so afraid they dare not wait for the cool?" he demanded once of his captors.

The Ute did not reply, but gave the old Comanche grim and angry looks. Twisted Foot found a certain pleasure in his own unspoken belief that the time would come when the Utes would regret the zeal that had prompted them to take Old Man Crazy as a captive, for Old Man Crazy was not an easy person to get along with, as the people of Kills Something's village had long since learned. Old Man Crazy was stubborn and quarrelsome. He was set in his ways and he had no regard for person or authority. He had no fear and he was never embarrassed. Even Kills Something, who was a stern and dominating leader, had become reluctant to cross him. All these things, together with his special standing with the great spirits because of his mental queerness, made him a very difficult and exasperating old man. And, as if this were not enough, he was a great eater, a nagging talker, and he refused to do any kind of work at all. Yes, the Utes would learn, Twisted Foot was certain, that they had gained nothing whatever in the way of comfort and tranquility for their village when they made a captive of Old Man Crazy. And in this, Twisted Foot, quite naturally, had not the slightest sympathy for them. On the contrary, he wished Old Man Crazy all success in creating all the dissatisfaction possible among them.

Near sundown, far farther into the big plains than Twisted Foot had ever been, the tall Ute signaled a halt.

There was a stream and the thirsty Indians threw themselves down at its side and sucked the water into their mouths. They made fires and broiled two long-eared rabbits that had been killed during the afternoon. They offered no food to the captives, but Old Man Crazy boldly tore a hind leg from one of the smoking carcasses.

"Are the Utes such poor hunters that this is all they have to offer?" he grumbled loudly. "Give the young Comanche his bow and arrows and he will kill a fat antelope for you." Old Man Crazy tore off a second rabbit leg and handed it to Twisted Foot, who would have gone hungry before asking for himself.

The Utes glared at Old Man Crazy, but none of them lifted a hand to stop him. Indeed, no one but one whose head was strange would act with such brazen assurance. The roasting flesh was too hot for the hand, but Old Man Crazy's fingers seemed not to feel the heat. He calmly tore off another leg for himself and ate it with great gusto, squatting on his lean old haunches. "It is not this ancient body but the hungry spirits that feed through my mouth," he told them. "Can you not see it is so?"

The Utes may have been uncertain as to that, but they waited no longer to divide the remainder of the rabbits between themselves.

Two more days, into a country big, strange and wide, they traveled steadily. Game was more abundant than Twisted Foot had ever thought possible. They frequently sighted buffalo. Antelope ran in herds. Grey wolves sat impudently at a distance and watched them. All kinds of birds and small animals were found along the water-courses. Twisted Foot could understand more clearly why the Utes fought so fiercely for this land.

On the third day they came to a large stream with an Indian village located among the trees that grew along the banks. Entrance of the little party into the village caused a flurry of noise and confusion. Dogs set up an outcry and almost immediately the three Utes and their captives were surrounded by women and children, all talking and shouting at once.

"Where are the others?"

"Was there a battle?"

"Were any killed?"

Old men and younger ones who had been left to guard the village came now and forced their way through the crowd. Twisted Foot noticed that in dress and looks these Utes were much like his own people, though possibly a little darker in hue of skin. Their language was different from his, and was difficult to understand, but he was beginning to recognize a few words, like "meat" and "fire."

"Are the Comanche dogs driven out?" one of the old men asked soberly.

"They flee," the tall warrior answered. "Our leader and his men are in pursuit. They will not rest as long as a Comanche remains in our country."

"Was there fighting?" another one asked.

[34]

The tall Ute shook his head. "The village was deserted
when we reached it. The Comanches are cowards. They
would not stay to fight. But the Ute warriors will be like
panthers on their trail. Those who escape will not be
eager to return to our prairie."

"But those who die will remain and their skins will
turn white. And they will move across the prairie at great
speed," Old Man Crazy said, speaking up unexpectedly
in his cracked old voice. "They will carry thunder and
lightning in their hands."

The Utes peered at Old Man Crazy's thin face and his
single glittering eye. One of them said, "Who is this, who
speaks of such impossible things? He should be left on
the prairie, sewn in a green hide to shrink with the heat
of the sun to consider his words and manners."

The tall warrior shook his head, somewhat sadly. "He is
a strange one," he said. "You will see. His fingers have no
feeling and queer things happen inside his head. We
found him alone at the Comanche village. He is like a
child that has no fear."

"The green hide might change all that," the old Ute
said darkly.

"No," Twisted Foot said firmly. "What the Ute warrior
says is true. The Comanches know the old one well. His
mind travels a dim trail."

"Bah!" Old Man Crazy cried impatiently. "Where are
the cooking fires? The spirits tell me they would eat. Later
you will hear more about the men with white skins." And

[35]

without further comment he marched through an aisle
that they opened for him to a fire where a paunch full of
meat hung cooking. With his bare hands he pulled out
a piece of the steaming flesh and began to eat.

The tall Ute looked at the others and shrugged helplessly. Then he said, "Come," to Twisted Foot and turned
through the crowd. Twisted Foot was relieved to get away
from those staring unfriendly eyes. The Ute led the way
to a large, brush-covered shelter. "This is my lodge," he
told Twisted Foot. "My wife will tell you what to do. If
you do not work well or if you try to escape, I will beat
you. The second time, I will kill you. Is it understood?"

"Yes," Twisted Foot said, well knowing the Ute meant
what he said.

The Ute turned into the wickiup and presently a woman
came out. She was a strong-bodied person with a dark
impassive face. She looked at Twisted Foot and her eyes
narrowed unpleasantly when she saw his deformed foot.
He knew what she was thinking—that he would be of
little value—but he was too tired and discouraged to care.
"Bring wood for the fire," the woman said.

The youth moved away toward the creek bottom, always the best source of wood at Indian camps. He drank
first, then went among the trees, picking up dry limbs and
branches. He gathered a big armful and took it back to
the lodge. The woman was cutting meat from a big hunk,
evidently to take inside to the hungry man, and she gave
Twisted Foot a thick juicy piece of it. He took it without

a word and ate it as he went back to the trees for more wood.

Later the woman gave him a thin, worn antelope robe and told him he could sleep in the lodge, at a place near the door. Twisted Foot tried to please her, knowing that if she complained, the tall Ute would beat him.

He brought wood for the fire, and water. He scraped hides and stretched them to dry, and others he rubbed with a paste of fat and brains and worked until they were soft and flexible. He made moccasins, a new pair to replace his own old worn ones as well as a better pair for the Ute. He cut meat into strips for the drying racks and crushed the marrow bones, not eating any of the rich marrow unless first given permission. No one appeared to be watching him, but he knew enough not to go far from the village, for a suspicion that he was trying to escape would result as unpleasantly as a real attempt, and when the time came for that, he did not intend that it should fail.

Twisted Foot saw Old Man Crazy frequently. The old Indian apparently moved about the village at will and seemed to be as much at home among the Utes as he had been among the Comanches. Sometimes he could be seen talking to little groups. The Utes listened with great interest but, like the Comanches, went away shaking their heads. Where Old Man Crazy slept and ate, Twisted Foot never learned, for Old Man Crazy in his ramblings did

[37]

not come near him and they had no opportunity to talk together.

One afternoon there was great excitement among the Utes and Twisted Foot learned that the war chief and his men were returning. Twisted Foot was among the crowd that gathered around the dusty braves. He listened intently as the chief told of their pursuit of the Comanches. "We drove them from the plains," the chief said. "I do not believe they will return. At the end they were greatly frightened, for they were throwing down their bundles and possessions."

"Were any killed?" one of the village old men asked.

"No," the leader said.

After that, Twisted Foot slipped away and back to his master's dwelling, for he did not want any of the Utes to see the happiness in his eyes.

A few days later the village moved, pushing on to another location where there was wood and water and game was plentiful. The young men went ahead with their bows and arrows to hunt, but Twisted Foot trudged among the women, carrying a heavy bundle. During the march he saw Old Man Crazy, hobbling along with a sleeping robe thrown across his bony shoulder.

The days became shorter and the weather turned windy and cold. Fires were built inside the lodges instead of in front of them, and Twisted Foot welcomed the nest of antelope hides in the tall Ute's shelter at night. Some days it was too cold and blizzardy to hunt, and they sat about the fires and ate dried meat. Then spring came, with its flourishing of new green grass and leaves, and Twisted Foot began to think seriously about escaping. This brought Old Man Crazy to his mind. He had seen little of the old Indian during the winter but knew he was still among the Utes, and it was in his mind to somehow work Old Man Crazy into his plans. Yet how to do it? He was not certain that the obstinate old Comanche would try to escape, even if an opportunity was offered.

Before Twisted Foot got far with his planning, however, something else happened. A Ute man returned to the village one afternoon in a state of high excitement. He had been hunting to the south with a companion and they had seen some strange, unknown and unnamed animals—animals with high heads and long necks and thick tails that dragged the grass. He was breathless in his description of them.

"Are you certain they were not elk?" the Ute chief questioned.

"I am certain," the man answered. "Does the hair on the upper neck of an elk grow so long as to reach its throat?"

Twisted Foot had seen the hunter hastening in and was now a short distance away, listening intently.

The Ute chief shook his head with some impatience. "There is no such animal," he said. "You walked too long under the sun."

The hunter, in turn, shook his head, and even more

vigorously. "They are true," he declared. "My companion killed one." His voice died away to a frightened half whisper.

"Killed one?" the chief repeated incredulously.

"Yes," the man said, trembling. "He hit it with an arrow. There were five of them, under a washed bank, and we were right above them before they saw us. There was a loud noise of the nose and thunder of the feet as they went away. I was too uncertain to move, but my companion sent an arrow."

Excitement spreads like measles in an Indian village and now the Utes were gathering, men and women and children. Twisted Foot got a glimpse of Old Man Crazy among them, and there was bright interest in Old Man Crazy's eye. "Were they by themselves?" Old Man Crazy asked.

"Yes, to be sure," the hunter said.

"Did you see no men with them?" Old Man Crazy asked.

"Men?" the hunter repeated. "Do not be more stupid than usual, old one."

"You say an arrow struck one down?" the Ute chief said to the hunter.

"Yes. It fell."

"It was likely an odd-shaped buffalo," one of the older wise men of the village said calmly. "I saw one like you describe once long ago. It was a buffalo. Later, I saw the man who killed it . . ."

"No," the hunter insisted stubbornly. "There is no hump. It has no horns. All of it is different. It is not like a deer or a bear or any other animal. I cannot understand it, my chief."

Twisted Foot was aware of keen inner excitement. He searched for Old Man Crazy again and saw that the old Indian had crowded forward to the front row of the circle and was listening with great intentness. Also there was a cunning and knowing glint in his eye.

"Take us to this place," the Ute chief ordered presently, "so we may see this strange thing that is like no other animal."

"I came for that purpose," the hunter said. "My companion stayed to make certain it did not disappear." He turned to lead the way.

A good portion of the village, including women and children, was in the excited group that followed the men out across the grassy plain. Twisted Foot was with them, his interest at a high pitch, and Old Man Crazy was too, hobbling along eagerly on his thin old legs. The chief and the village wise men were up in the front rank, and most of them were openly skeptical of the story. One kept insisting that it would prove to be only a buffalo, and another thought it was surely an elk, such as he had seen in the forested foothill regions to the north. "The females," this man said, "have no hump or horns. And there is hair on the neck. You will see."

Before they reached the place, however, a man appeared

[41]

on the prairie and came running swiftly toward them. The leaders halted, concerned. And their concern increased when it could be seen, as the runner drew closer, that he was greatly excited and frightened, and also that he was limping.

"It is my companion," the hunter who had brought the news said.

"Why does he hasten so?" the chief asked. "Why did he not remain?"

"I do not know," the hunter answered uneasily.

They waited for the man to come up. His face was flustered and he was out of breath. "One came back!" he gasped to them. "It attacked me!"

"One of the strange beasts?" the chief cried.

"Yes," the man said.

"How did it attack you?" the chief asked. "He said that it has no horns."

"That is true," the man panted. "But it has mighty feet. I was sitting by the one that was killed when suddenly a fierce one returned. Look at this hurt on my thigh." He half turned to show them a large bruise, already red and inflamed. "It did that with its foot. It would have eaten me also, had I not fled, for it came at me with its mouth open. See the gashes on my back. Even the great panthers are meek by comparison to it. It is a beast of the evil spirits, my brothers. I fear we have offended it."

This increased the excitement and the concern among

the Utes. The chief and the old wise men immediately went into a council to determine what should be done. Old Man Crazy edged forward to listen, and Twisted Foot found a place close behind him.

"There is great danger," one of the old men said solemnly. "My medicine has warned me that this might happen."

"But we must continue," the chief said. "It is better that we meet it here on the plains than have it come in the night to our village. It could kill many of us while we slept."

"Perhaps it would be better if we moved the village to another place," another old man said. "We could move secretly, at night."

The hunter who had remained at the scene of the kill shook his head dolefully and said, "It is a beast of the evil spirits."

"True," an old man said accusingly. "You should have held your arrow. You have brought danger to us all."

"But then I did not know," the man cried plaintively. "I believed it to be meat, that our people could eat. I did not know it had a breath of fire."

This discussion continued for some time, during which the chief and the old men weighed the problem with great seriousness. Some were for returning to the village for their spears and war clubs and marching as a war party against the strange creatures.

"That will accomplish nothing," Old Man Crazy told

[43]

them, speaking up suddenly. "You will not see the beasts again, not until it is too late. Their flight is as swift as that of an eagle and they strike with the suddenness of the lightning. I speak with true knowledge for I have seen them, not one but many. When they are angered, they crush all that is in their path. Ask this man." He pointed to the crestfallen hunter. "He will tell you."

The hunter, now sitting weakly on the ground, did not have the courage to look up at them.

"He speaks the truth," one of the old men said positively. "My medicine has warned me. I know it now. Next time the evil spirits may appear in a different form. It is bad that we have offended them."

The chief considered this for several seconds, and when he spoke it was with reluctance. "You must leave the tribe," he said to the hunter on the ground. "If you remain you will bring misfortune on us all."

"And the other with him," one of the old men said approvingly. "He too is at fault, for he saw the shape of the evil spirits. They will not rest while he lives."

"Yes," the chief said. "Go," he ordered the two men. "Go until you are far away. Do not halt in Ute country. And do not come again to our village." His voice was stern and he lifted his hand and pointed to the horizon.

The people pulled back from the two men and divided to leave a path for them. Slowly the man on the ground got to his feet. He did not look at the people but started away, walking with miserable and reluctant steps, his dark head shamefully down. The chief turned his stern gaze on the second hunter. This man glanced about for signs of sympathy. "It is to protect our people," the chief told him. "Your wife will be told, that she may follow if she wishes. But do not come again to Ute country."

The hunter started after the other, and they went straight across the plains until they passed over a crest and out of sight.

The chief stirred and turned to the crowd. "Return at once to your lodges and prepare to move," he said. "We will leave this place in the night. When the sun comes again, we will be gone."

The people turned back toward the village and began hurrying over the dry grass, anxious now to be about the preparations for moving. A number cast frightened glances over their shoulders, as if fearing pursuit by the evil spirits. Clouds in the sky added a doleful touch by cutting off the light, and the women scurried like startled prairie quail before a wolf.

Twisted Foot moved until he was at the side of Old Man Crazy, who was hurrying as if he were as alarmed as the others. "Do you believe it to be the shape of an evil spirit?" Twisted Foot asked in a guarded voice.

"To be certain. Shame on you. Do you wish to be killed?" Old Man Crazy replied loudly. "Hasten to the village and pack your master's belongings." But there was a bright cunning in Old Man Crazy's eye that caused Twisted Foot to wonder.

[45]

The village was soon all astir with the business of moving. Twisted Foot helped the women fasten the travois poles on the dogs and load the numerous bundles. The dogs lay down between the poles to rid themselves of the weight until it was time to start. Twisted Foot helped make packs to be carried by the women and by himself. But all the time he was thinking about the strangeness that had been in Old Man Crazy's manner.

Just before dark, Old Man Crazy, who had been wandering about and adding to the anxiety and confusion, passed near Twisted Foot. "When the moving starts," he said in a low voice, "go to the plum thicket. Secure a knife and the best bow you can find, and a quiver of arrows."

"The plum . . ." Twisted Foot repeated to be certain he had heard correctly.

But Old Man Crazy was already moving on. "This happened once before," he said loudly to any who would listen. "A Comanche village is no more. It was I alone that escaped."

It was dark when the chief and the old men gathered at the edge of the village and gave the signal to start. The women and children got under their packs and bundles, and everyone began shouting at the dogs. The dogs struggled up in their travois poles and the movement began, filtering slowly through the fringe of trees and into the gloom of the prairie.

Twisted Foot picked up the pack he had made for him-

self. It had the tall Ute's spare bow and a quiver of good arrows tied to it. He got it on his back and moved after the women, but in the darkness he gradually fell behind. Presently he angled off to the right and continued in that direction until he was alone. Then he made a wide circle through the grass that brought him back to the plum thicket.

In the thicket it was very dark and Twisted Foot approached cautiously, wondering how much confidence he dared place in the strange quirks of Old Man Crazy's mind. It was well known that the old Indian was often foolish to the point of danger.

"Come in, little brother, and let your burden down," Old Man Crazy's voice said calmly.

Twisted Foot went among the trees. Old Man Crazy was resting on a bed robe.

"This is the time to escape," Twisted Foot said excitedly. "We will go at once. By the time they know we are not with them we will be far away. I do not think they can catch us."

"Make your bed, little brother," Old Man Crazy said. "I am too old to run, from the Utes or any others. Did you bring a bow and arrows?"

"Yes," Twisted Foot said. "But we must hurry or they will catch us again. They can travel faster."

Old Man Crazy snorted disdainfully. "Think," he said. "What is the one place to which the Utes will not come? What is the place they even now flee from in fear?"

Twisted Foot thought, then, somewhat abashed, said, "This place, old man. You have more wisdom than I."

Old Man Crazy chuckled and said, "That is not surprising, little brother, for I likewise have many more years. While we stay here, we are safe."

Twisted Foot pulled his sleeping robe out of his bundle. "But what about the evil spirits?" he inquired. "Are you not afraid of them?"

"Yes," Old Man Crazy said. "But not those that were seen today. Those were not evil spirits, little brother; those were horses."

"Horses?" Twisted Foot cried softly, marveling.

"Yes," Old Man Crazy said. "You have heard me tell of them before. I saw them with the men with the white skins."

"The men who lived inside the hard shells?" Twisted Foot said.

"Yes," Old Man Crazy answered.

"But if the horses are here, where are the men?" Twisted Foot asked.

Several seconds passed before Old Man Crazy replied. "That I cannot tell, little brother," he said. "It is something to think about."

Twisted Foot remembered all the many things that had happened during that day and he remembered the ugly bruise that had been on the hunter's back. "Even if they are not evil spirits, old man," he said presently, "they will hurt people. They attacked the hunter."

[49]

"Sometimes they do, and sometimes not," Old Man Crazy said. "They never attacked the men with the white skins. They even permitted them to ride on their backs."

Twisted Foot shook his head and said, "I cannot understand it, father."

"At first I could not believe it either, but it is true," Old Man Crazy said. "And on their backs the men with the white skins could move faster than any man can run."

"Faster than any man can run?" Twisted Foot echoed unbelievingly.

"Yes," Old Man Crazy said. "I saw it. Now go to sleep. Tomorrow we will think about it some more." He turned over on his robe and was soon snoring.

But it was not easy for Twisted Foot to go to sleep. The words *faster than any man can run* kept going through his mind over and over again. *Faster than any man can run.* Of course he could not run very fast, because of his deformed foot but . . . *faster than any man can run . . . faster . . .*

CHAPTER FOUR

THE SUN was up when Twisted Foot awoke the next morning. He rolled to his knees, crawled to the edge of the thicket and looked out. The area was as the Utes had left it. Twisted Foot saw abandoned brush wickiups and drying racks. Blackened spots told where the fires had been and well-beaten foot trails threaded the trees to the areas of wood and water. Twisted Foot was half afraid a Ute, come back to search for them, might be there, but none appeared. The only movement was that of an old gray badger sniffing about the dead ashes.

"I would eat," Old Man Crazy said from his bed. "In the house of the one who wore three feathers I think there is a piece of cooked meat."

Twisted Foot remembered the big Ute who habitually wore three long feathers in his hair. He left the thicket and went to this man's hut. A big chunk of broiled meat was suspended from the low roof.

Old Man Crazy was waiting with his piece of sharpened stone when Twisted Foot returned to the thicket. He cut a slice of the meat and began to eat. Twisted Foot cut

some meat for himself and wondered how Old Man Crazy
had known the meat was in the hut. He did not ask, however, for he did not wish to seem to be prying into the
secrets of a strange one. The meat was good and they
ate all they could comfortably hold, which was customary
with the Indians of that day because they were never
certain of when the next opportunity would come.
Twisted Foot wrapped the meat that was left in a piece of
buckskin to show that it belonged to them.

"How long will we remain on this plain, old man?" he
asked.

"As long as we wish," Old Man Crazy said. "It will be
a long time before the Utes return to this spot."

"I would like to be in Kill Something's village again,"
Twisted Foot said. "It would be good to see my father and
mother, and my brothers and sisters. Are you not anxious
to return to the village also?"

Old Man Crazy nodded. "There is time for that. I am
thinking now of a thing that is of great importance."

"Is not getting back to our people important?" Twisted
Foot asked.

"No," Old Man Crazy said.

Twisted Foot did not understand this but he said nothing more, being somewhat timid of interrupting the old
Indian's thoughts. Since he was a strange one and knew
about the spirits, Old Man Crazy might be thinking of
unheard-of things.

And it seemed as if Old Man Crazy was, for presently
he muttered, "Sometimes they walked beside them, and at

other times it was as if the two were only one. And there was fire and thunder in the skies."

Twisted Foot waited a time for Old Man Crazy to say more, but Old Man Crazy didn't. Twisted Foot asked, "What?" timidly, wondering what Old Man Crazy could be talking about.

Old Man Crazy did not seem to hear, for he did not answer. Twisted Foot did not ask again.

For quite some time Old Man Crazy sat there, a lean old Indian hunched under his robe, his thick hair falling over his shoulders and his single eye staring unseeingly at the crooked trunks of the plum trees. He was visibly so deep in the peculiar things of his own mind that Twisted Foot sat still and silent.

"Men fell down at a distance and were no more," Old Man Crazy said.

Twisted Foot could make nothing of this either. More long minutes passed. Finally, Old Man Crazy pushed himself to his feet. "It is a thing of great importance, little brother," he said. "Come. And bring the meat."

They left the plum thicket and started across the plains, the old man in front, Twisted Foot behind with his bow and arrows, carrying what was left of the meat, still wrapped in the piece of buckskin. Old Man Crazy walked slowly but steadily, his robe over his shoulder, and there was a new dignity of purpose in his manner.

"Where do we go, father?" Twisted Foot asked presently.

"I have not fully determined yet," Old Man Crazy said.

[53]

"The village of our people is in the ravine country," Twisted Foot reminded hopefully.

Old Man Crazy apparently did not hear him.

A little later Twisted Foot asked, "Is it not likely the Utes may see us out here, father? I do not wish to be a captive again."

Old Man Crazy said, "Watch sharply, little brother, and tell me at once if you see a man, or any creature larger than an antelope. There may be danger greater than the Utes."

Twisted Foot wondered, but asked no further questions. He knew they were in the area where the strange animal had been killed, and he began to feel somewhat disturbed. What if, after all, it was an evil spirit? He doubted that he, with his crippled foot, and Old Man Crazy, with his puzzled head, would be a match for it.

Old Man Crazy kept on steadily, and Twisted Foot stayed close behind him. Eventually they came to the lip of a dry wash. Old Man Crazy hesitated and looked down into the wash. Impelled by curiosity, Twisted Foot moved up to where he could see.

"It is not there," Twisted Foot said quickly. "It *has* disappeared."

"We are not at the place," Old Man Crazy said calmly. "Look along the wash."

They went along the winding lip and Twisted Foot watched the bottom. Presently he saw something, an animal, lying on its side. "There is something," he said, pointing.

Old Man Crazy hurried forward and in a few seconds they were on the lip above the creature. Twisted Foot had never seen such an animal before. "Is it a horse?" he asked dubiously.

Old Man Crazy nodded.

"But it is not as big as you said," Twisted Foot told him. "It is not as tall as an elk. It is not much bigger than an antelope."

"It is small," Old Man Crazy said, "but it is a horse. I have seen them before. It is a young one, like a fawn."

"It has no spots," Twisted Foot said. "A fawn would have spots."

"No," Old Man Crazy admitted, "but it is a young one. It is because of that the Ute had opportunity to kill it. Grown ones run very fast."

"One came back," Twisted Foot pointed out.

"Likely it was the mother of the young one," Old Man Crazy said. "We know such things happen."

"Is the horse kin to the bear or the panther?" Twisted Foot asked, wondering.

"No, but it will sometimes fight for its young as they do," Old Man Crazy said. He slid down the bank, closer to the animal. "See," he went on, "it has a hoof, not a paw. It has hair, not fur. Nor does it have the long fangs of a meat-eater. It is of the family of the grass-eaters."

[55]

"Its feet are very strange," Twisted Foot said. "They have no toes."

"That is true," Old Man Crazy said. "But they can run very fast."

Twisted Foot remembered ... *faster than any man can run*. And with the men with the white skins on their backs. It seemed impossible.

"How do the men with the white skins get on their backs, father?" he asked presently. "What keeps them from falling off?"

"They jump up, and they hold on," Old Man Crazy said.

"But how?" Twisted Foot persisted. "Do the men lie on their backs?"

"No. They stand up, with one leg on each side, like a man astride a log," Old Man Crazy answered.

"Are their legs long enough to reach the ground?" Twisted Foot wanted to know, his eyes widening.

"No," Old Man Crazy said impatiently. "Come. It is time we left this place." He crossed the wash and climbed the sloping bank, back to the level of the plain. He paused here and asked, "Do you see anything, little brother? The distance is not clear to my eye."

"Only some antelope," Twisted Foot said. "And off yonder," he added, pointing, "are some wolves, three, I think, but possibly only two. The third may be a badger they are worrying. Will they eat the horse, father?"

"Yes," Old Man Crazy said. "That is good, for then other eyes will not see it."

"Why is that important, father?" Twisted Foot asked.

"It is best if the Utes continue to believe they are evil spirits," Old Man Crazy answered. "Do you see the others of which the hunter told?"

Twisted Foot looked again and said, "I do not see any."

Old Man Crazy stood for several minutes with his thoughts turned inward. "I wish," he said, "my legs had the suppleness and endurance they once had, and my arms the strength."

"Why, father?" Twisted Foot asked.

"There is a thing I would do," Old Man Crazy replied with some bitterness.

"Perhaps I can do it," Twisted Foot said.

Old Man Crazy turned and looked at the youth, his one eye speculating. He glanced downward at the deformed foot.

Twisted Foot put the foot back, so it was partly hidden by the other. "I am not weak," he said firmly. "You will learn that, father."

Old Man Crazy still hesitated and several seconds passed. He said, "There were five, did not the Ute say?"

"Five?" Twisted Foot repeated, puzzled.

"Five horses," Old Man Crazy snapped. "Are your ears closed?"

"Yes, father," Twisted Foot said humbly. "He said five."

"Then, find the other four," Old Man Crazy ordered. "I would see them."

"But, father . . ."

Old Man Crazy interrupted him impatiently. "They cannot fly," he said. "They leave marks on the ground. Are your eyes no better than mine?"

"Yes, father," Twisted Foot said, and immediately he began to search the grass for the round tracks, heartened by the knowledge that they would be unmistakable. After a time he found them. "Here is the sign, father. Come this way."

"Good," Old Man Crazy grunted.

Twisted Foot moved in the lead and Old Man Crazy followed. The youth went slowly, for the trail, in the dry grass, needed all of his tracking skill. Often there were only thin bent blades to follow. "It is a faint trail, father," he said after a time, afraid that he was not going fast enough to please the old Indian.

"A faint trail well followed is as true as a plain one," Old Man Crazy answered, surprisingly patient now.

Twisted Foot gave all of his attention to the sign, watching for the bent or crushed blades and the small abrasions in the dry soil. He moved bent well forward, and Old Man Crazy trudged behind him. They were two small dark figures on the great plain, insignificant in the country's vastness.

The sun burned on across the wide dome of the sky and presently went behind the western horizon. Twisted Foot straightened up. "I can no longer follow, father," he said.

"Where is the trail?" Old Man Crazy asked sternly.

"It is here," Twisted Foot said, pointing to the grass. "But the light is gone."

Old Man Crazy threw his robe to the ground. "We will stay here until it is light again. Where is the meat?"

Twisted Foot unwrapped the meat and Old Man Crazy cut a slice and began to eat. Twisted Foot cut a piece for himself. It was a good-sized chunk from the leg of an antelope and, slice by slice, they ate it to the bone. Twisted Foot then hunted a rock with which to crack the bone, and they ate the tasty marrow, running their tongues along the grooves.

Old Man Crazy sighed with contentment and lay back on his robe. Twisted Foot spread his own robe. The night was warm and the grass was soft. There was a dry musty smell in the air. Stars appeared in unbelievable numbers in the wide, dark expanse of the sky. Far off a coyote howled and the clear faint sound was immediately caught up by others.

Water would have been welcome, but neither the old man nor the youth mentioned it. There was no water, so why talk about it? Tomorrow they would find a stream or a water hole.

Lying there and watching the stars, Twisted Foot wondered about Old Man Crazy. The old Indian was no longer his talkative and scornfully indifferent self. He had changed, had become touchy and irritable and secretive. He obviously had something on his mind, something important. Twisted Foot had the feeling that the old man

[59]

was a stranger, someone he had never known before, of much more worth and importance than Old Man Crazy. He could not entirely understand his feeling and was somewhat awed.

"We will keep after the sign," Old Man Crazy said, as if thinking aloud.

"Yes, father," Twisted Foot said softly.

"We will see them," Old Man Crazy went on.

Twisted Foot did not reply and a silence followed.

"We must get close," Old Man Crazy said. "But we must not scare them. Do you hear that, little brother? We must not scare them."

"Yes, father," Twisted Foot said.

Old Man Crazy grunted and turned on his side. He lay that way awhile, then turned on his back. After a time, his voice as soft as Twisted Foot had ever heard it, he asked, "Are you afraid, little brother?"

Afraid? Twisted Foot didn't know. He had a strange feeling but he had not thought it was fear. He said, "No, father. I am not afraid."

"That is good," Old Man Crazy said, a mystifying tone in his voice.

Twisted Foot thought awhile, then asked, "Is it the Utes? Do you fear they will find us?"

"The Utes! Bah!" Old Man Crazy snorted. "They are women who run from their shadows. They know nothing."

[60]

"Then," Twisted Foot asked, "what is there to fear, father?"

Old Man Crazy was a long time in replying, then he said, "We will have a horse."

The stars above Twisted Foot's head suddenly wheeled in dizzying arcs. Have a horse! He and Old Man Crazy alone . . . ? The old Comanche was having another of his foolish dreams.

CHAPTER FIVE

THEY HAD NO breakfast, but that was of little concern
to these Comanches. They would make up for it
when the next opportunity offered. They got up from
the ground, picked up their robes and threw them over
their shoulders, and were ready to travel, leaving nothing
behind, needing nothing else.

"Can you make out the trail, little brother?" Old Man
Crazy asked with enthusiasm.

"Yes. Here they were eating."

"Eating?" Old Man Crazy said. "Let me see. Where?"

"At this place," Twisted Foot said, kneeling at a tuft
of grass that had been bitten halfway to the roots.

Old Man Crazy squinted and felt the short blades with
his fingers. "It is as I believed," he said. "Grass is their
food."

"Yes," Twisted Foot agreed. "I have seen nothing in
their droppings to show that they eat flesh."

"Continue the sign," Old Man Crazy said.

For a distance the trail was difficult, for the animals
had separated and wandered and moved in circles, and

much of the grass had been eaten. Old Man Crazy was impatient while Twisted Foot searched back and forth. After a time the youth made a wide cast and soon discovered a straight-away sign. He signaled to Old Man Crazy to follow, but Old Man Crazy could not see him at that distance. He went back and called to Old Man Crazy. "Here is the trail, father."

A long time later, in the distance, Twisted Foot saw a line of green trees and brush. "The sign is leading to water," he said.

Old Man Crazy nodded. "It is the custom of the grass-eaters," he said. "After they eat, they need to drink. Then perhaps they will sleep. The sun is so hot they will likely seek the shade. Do you see any antelope, little brother?"

"Antelope?" Twisted Foot repeated, with some surprise.

"Yes."

Twisted Foot looked around and presently on a crest saw a pointed head with the peculiarly curving black horns. "There are some antelope," he said.

"We need one," Old Man Crazy said. "I will wait here." He dropped his robe to the ground.

Twisted Foot moved in the direction of the antelope. Soon he saw more heads, and white-barred necks. He found a place where there was some cover and sat down. He took two arrows from his quiver, and to one he attached a piece of white buckskin. He fixed this above his head, so the buckskin would flutter in the wind. It was

[63]

not long after that he heard the antelope running. They ran along the crest, a good herd of them, then turned and swung wide to his left. They halted and stood with heads and ears alert, looking at the piece of buckskin. Suddenly they were off again, running, but in a wide circle. Once more they stopped and stamped their small feet in puzzlement and curiosity. Then their light yellow forms stretched in great leaps across the prairie.

This went on for some time, the fleet animals running and halting alternately, but in their impelling curiosity working closer and closer to the fluttering flag. Twisted Foot sat and thought about Old Man Crazy and wondered if he were wise in listening to the old Indian. He knew that Kills Something and his father did not have much regard for Old Man Crazy, that they considered him as being puzzled and uncertain in his mind. They believed that the stories he told were the results of dreams, and Twisted Foot had believed it also. Now, however, he wasn't sure. The strange animals the old man had talked about so much did exist. Of this, Twisted Foot was certain. The Ute hunters had seen them, and he had seen one also, though it was a dead one. But to capture one? He shook his head, doubting that it could be done. With his crippled foot he could not run fast; and Old Man Crazy could not run, or see very well either. How could Old Man Crazy expect them to catch a horse? The experience of the Ute hunters had proved that the animals were wild and dangerous . . .

[64]

Twisted Foot pulled his bowstring back to his chin and let the arrow fly. It went deep into the neck of a fat young antelope. The rest of the herd whirled and fled, their white rumps flashing brilliantly in the sun. Twisted Foot opened and bled the one he had killed, then pushed it up on his shoulder and carried it back to where Old Man Crazy waited. They ate the liver and some of the meat, then Old Man Crazy got to his feet and said, "We will go now. Follow the sign, little brother."

Twisted Foot carried the antelope and they made their way on across the prairie, following the trail left by the horses. They were still some distance from the trees when Old Man Crazy told him to halt. "Where does the trail lead now?" Old Man Crazy asked.

"It leads that way," Twisted Foot said, pointing toward the nearest trees.

Old Man Crazy wet a finger and tested the direction of the wind. Twisted Foot knew from this that there was feeling in the old man's hands after all. His tearing apart the hot meat had been a trick. Old Man Crazy had more sense than people thought.

"We will go to the stream yonder," Old Man Crazy said. He pointed off at an angle and Twisted Foot knew it was the old Indian's plan to reach the cover on the downwind side of the horses, if they were among the trees.

They moved on in the direction Old Man Crazy had chosen, and, as they approached the trees, Old Man Crazy said, "Watch closely and keep your bow ready, little brother." Twisted Foot knew that Old Man Crazy was more nervous than he would admit. Twisted Foot was nervous too, not knowing but that one of the strange beasts might leap out at him at any instant.

However, they reached the trees without anything unusual happening. In the shade Twisted Foot paused and looked about carefully. Two deer, moving gracefully between the trunks as they slipped away, gave him a start.

"Do you see anything, little brother?" Old Man Crazy questioned anxiously.

"No," Twisted Foot said.

They went on to the water and lay down and drank. After that, they sat for some time on the grassy bank, watching and listening. A dark-brown beaver climbed dripping from the water, waddled to a fallen cottonwood tree and began feeding on the tender bark of an upper limb.

The beaver had eaten its fill and gone back to the water when Old Man Crazy spoke. "They are upstream," he said, half a statement and half a question.

Twisted Foot said nothing. He had followed Old Man Crazy's reasoning, but still he didn't know. There was no assurance that these strange animals could be stalked like deer or buffalo.

"We will find them," Old Man Crazy said. "But they must not see us."

Twisted Foot agreed, but did not speak.

"We must move silently and watch closely," Old Man Crazy said.

"The trees are close together," Twisted Foot said.

"When I had two eyes, I could see through trees," Old Man Crazy snapped irritably.

"Yes, father," Twisted Foot said, humbled.

More minutes passed, with no sound except the drone of flying insects. Finally and reluctantly, Old Man Crazy pushed to his feet. "We will go now, little brother," he said. "I will carry the meat, so you may keep your bow ready." He shouldered what was left of the antelope.

Twisted Foot started through the trees, using all his skill for silence and carefully searching with his eyes. The cover was so dense that in places he could see no more than a few yards, and he halted frequently to sniff the air and listen. He saw another beaver, using its flat tail as a prop while it worked with its long orange-colored teeth on the trunk of a young tree. He circled around the animal to keep from startling it, not knowing what ears might hear the warning slap of its tail if it dived back into the water. A rabbit flushed from a hiding place and scuttled away through the undergrowth. Twisted Foot stood in fixed silence until all noise of the flight had died away. Old Man Crazy waited too, well knowing the value of patience now. On they went, two dark intent figures moving stealthily through the brush and shadows.

Half an hour or more had passed when Twisted Foot suddenly halted and became tense. He was still for a second, then whispered, "I smell animals, father."

"It is likely them," Old Man Crazy said, crowding up close. "Look carefully, little brother."

Twisted Foot surveyed every visible inch of the leafy cover. "I cannot see anything," he said. "They must be hiding."

Old Man Crazy lowered the antelope, carefully, so that it made no sound. "Crawl," he whispered.

They got down on their stomachs and inched through the brush. Twisted Foot pushed his bow ahead with his left hand. Presently they approached a little shaded opening, not far from a still pool in the stream. Twisted Foot's heart leaped into his throat. What he had first thought to be four young trees were legs and through the leaves he could make out a shape, astoundingly big. He gave Old Man Crazy a warning dig with his foot. This was a horse; something told him so instantly.

The tall shape did not move. Its head was drooping and its attitude was one of resting. Twisted Foot became aware of another one, to the right, and still another one behind the second. He was surprised by their colors. They were shaped alike, undoubtedly of the same animal family, but their colors varied amazingly. The one he had seen first was reddish brown, with darker neck and tail, and on its head, in the high center, there was a splash of white. One of the others was as black as night, with no white whatever, and the third one was gray, the color of the shale back in the ravine country. All had thick hair growing at the tops of their necks and long dense tails, tails unlike those of any other animal he had ever seen.

There was a silent movement beside him as Old Man

Crazy pulled up. Old Man Crazy's one eye could make out the animals at that distance and he lay there, studying them intently.

Twisted Foot could feel his heart pounding with excitement. Here were the strange and wonderful creatures which Old Man Crazy had told about—the horses of the men with white skins. They did not appear as ferocious and dangerous as he had expected. They were big, however, bigger than he had thought, even from Old Man Crazy's wild descriptions. He studied them carefully, legs, bodies, necks and heads. He knew enough about animals to see that one was a male, a stallion, and the other two were mares, females. The stallion was the brown one with the white spot. The coat of the black one was dusty, even high on her back. The gray one was thick-bodied and her milk glands were tight and swollen, indicating that she was the mother of the young one the Ute had killed.

A sudden movement almost caused Twisted Foot to leap from his hiding place under the bushes. Something heaved up from the ground between him and the horses, something big and black. He expected the horses to start, but they paid no attention. Then he saw what it was— another horse, one that had been lying down.

Gaining its feet, this new horse shook itself mightily, sending out a small spray of dust and leaves. It too was black, with a small white spot on its forehead. It did not seem as big as the others, and its mane and tail were shorter. Twisted Foot reached the conclusion that it was younger, not yet grown, though already larger and heavier-boned than the biggest deer. Like the brown horse, this one was a male.

While Twisted Foot and Old Man Crazy watched, the young stallion went to the stream's edge and drank, the gulps of water running smoothly up his long neck. Like all grass-eaters, he drank with his muzzle in the water and when he raised his head, water dribbled from his mouth, the drops sparkling in the sun. Twisted Foot noticed that his body was strong and well-rounded, with a gracefully curving line of the back entirely different from the humps of the buffalo or the thick straight backs of the deer and antelope.

The other horses stirred now and the two Indians lay very still. The brown stallion went to the stream and drank deeply. He lifted his head, looked about, and then drank a second time. He turned and moved leisurely through the clearing and went on through the trees and brush, out to the grassy plain. A moment or two later the mares drank and went to join the stallion. The young black horse followed them.

Twisted Foot let the excited breath out of his lungs slowly. "Horses are very big animals, father," he said.

"They are very strong also," Old Man Crazy said. "Did you notice their backs? They are of a shape to carry things. One can carry as much as ten dogs."

"Did you say," Twisted Foot asked, "they carried the

men with the white skins on their backs? And without protesting?"

"I saw it, little brother," Old Man Crazy answered. "I saw them carry the men with white skins at great speed, like the buffalo when they are frightened."

"How did the men come back?" Twisted Foot wanted to know. "Did they walk?"

Old Man Crazy shook his head. "No. The horses brought them back."

"Do you mean the horses took them wherever they wished to go?" Twisted Foot asked, finding it difficult to believe.

"Yes," Old Man Crazy said positively. "That is what they did."

"But how," Twisted Foot asked, deeply puzzled, "did the men with the white skins tell the horses where they wished to go? Can the men with the white skins speak in a language the horses understand?"

Old Man Crazy thought about that for several seconds before he answered. "Yes," he said. "I did not hear them talk, but I saw it. The horses understood."

CHAPTER SIX

FROM THE MANY tracks and droppings it was evident to Twisted Foot and Old Man Crazy that the horses they had seen had been much in this small opening and along the stream bank. "They have been here to drink and rest many times," Old Man Crazy said. "It is good. They will come again. We will go down the stream a safe distance to make our fire."

They went through the trees, in the direction they had come, but now not so cautiously. Twisted Foot took up the meat Old Man Crazy had dropped. They found a secluded place near the water where a toppled tree offered an abundance of dry wood. Twisted Foot made a fire and Old Man Crazy cut the meat in chunks for cooking. They suspended small pieces of the meat on green sticks over the coals, and there wasn't much talking until after they had filled their lean stomachs.

Old Man Crazy stretched out on his sleeping robe, though it was several hours yet until dark. "Under the men with the white skins," he said thoughtfully, "the horses changed their points of direction quickly, even while moving at great speed. They would be going one way and suddenly would turn to another. Also they would stop and stand still at the will of the men. Even they would go backward. Once I saw it."

Twisted Foot shook his head. "It is difficult to believe, father," he said.

"It is true," Old Man Crazy declared, a bit testily. "And why should it be so difficult to understand? They have ears, just as do our dogs. Our dogs understand our words. They will come at our call and follow at our command. You have often seen it."

"But horses are so big and strong," Twisted Foot said. "Do the men with the white skins dare punish them to make them obey as we do our dogs?"

Old Man Crazy shrugged and said, "I do not know. But they did obey."

Twisted Foot was silent for several seconds, then said, "I wish I knew the language of the men with the white skins, father."

"That is impossible," Old Man Crazy said. "Even I do not know it, and I have seen the men."

Twisted Foot was seated on the robe that he carried to sleep on or under, as the weather indicated. He said, "I do not know then how we can ever make them understand us."

"I am hopeful," Old Man Crazy said thoughtfully. "Did you not notice in the Ute village that the dogs understood the Utes, though the language is not the same as

Comanche? Is it not possible that horses, as well as dogs, can learn a different tongue? Or a new one? Is it not possible that they might learn the words of the Comanche?"

Twisted Foot thought, then asked, "But how, father? We can not teach them, even though they would learn, unless they will listen. We can not teach them while they run, either from us or toward us. And until they know, there is no way they can understand what we would tell them."

Old Man Crazy nodded in agreement and said, "We must make them listen."

"But how can we do that?" Twisted Foot wanted to know.

"I have not yet thought it out," Old Man Crazy said with a snappishness that indicated he did not wish to discuss the matter further at this time.

Twisted Foot let the silence run on for several minutes, but there was so much excitement in him that he could not repress himself for long. "Where are the men with the white skins, father?" he asked. "How is it that their horses are here but they are not?"

Old Man Crazy shrugged and said, "The men did not come."

"But why? Why did they not come?" Twisted Foot asked. "Why did they let the horses come without them?"

"I do not claim to know everything," Old Man Crazy said, his manner brusque. "The horses are here. I have seen nothing of the men with the white skins. Perhaps they did not wish to come. It is many days of walking to the place where I saw them."

"But if they did not wish to come, why did they permit the horses to come without them, father?" Twisted Foot persisted. "Why did not they keep the horses at that place also?"

"Why is that important?" Old Man Crazy said. "Perhaps they did come, but have gone back."

"Then why did they leave the horses?" Twisted Foot asked. "Are the horses of so little value to them?"

"No," Old Man Crazy said. "The horses are of great value to them. That I know, little brother. They guard them carefully. Indians were not permitted to go near them."

"Perhaps that is why the horses are afraid of us," Twisted Foot said. "They do not know us."

"That could be true," Old Man Crazy agreed. "Also it is in my mind that the men with the white skins have taught the horses not to like us."

"Why would they do that?" Twisted Foot asked.

"I think it is because they do not want Indians to have a horse," Old Man Crazy said. "It is their wish to keep all horses for themselves."

"Then why did they leave them?" Twisted Foot said. "I do not understand it."

"They did not leave them willingly," Old Man Crazy said. "Of that, I am certain. It is possible the horses escaped."

[76]

"Escaped?" Twisted Foot repeated. "Would they leave the men with the white skins?"

"Yes," Old Man Crazy said. "The men with the white skins kept long ropes on their necks to prevent that when it was necessary to put them on the grass. I will make a rope, little brother. I will make a fine rope for us."

"But if the horses escaped, would not the men with the white skins follow them and catch them again?" Twisted Foot asked. "Would they not do that?"

"Yes," Old Man Crazy admitted, grumbling.

"Then where are they? Why are they not here? Why are there no ropes about the horses' necks?"

"Can you not rest?" Old Man Crazy cried with sudden sharpness. "Who can say concerning that without knowing? Do you doubt that the horses are here?"

"No, father," Twisted Foot said. "But where are the men?"

Old Man Crazy did not answer but flopped over on his robe and appeared to go to sleep. Twisted Foot gazed up at the leaves and at the patches of blue sky that filled in between them. He wondered if they could ever catch one of the horses and make it understand Comanche. The thought was keenly exciting, but he could foresee many difficulties, some of which just didn't, at that time, have any solution. It would, however, be wonderful to have a horse, especially so because of his crippled foot. With a horse to do his bidding, he would no longer need to worry about his foot, for a horse could carry him *faster than any man can run*.

"How do the men with the white skins keep from falling, father?" he asked before remembering Old Man Crazy's irritable mood.

Old Man Crazy rolled over on his back. "They stayed on," he said shortly.

Perhaps, Twisted Foot thought, it was not so difficult after all. If he could get his arms around the horse's neck, that would help. He wished his legs were longer, so they would go around the horse's body too.

Another question came to him. "Did the men with the white skins have many horses, father? Was there a horse for each of them?"

"No," Old Man Crazy said. "There were many more men with white skins than horses. But there may have been more horses than I saw. It was the chiefs whom the horses carried."

"Did you see these—the horses we saw at the opening?" Twisted Foot asked.

"I do not know," Old Man Crazy said. "I cannot remember. I do not think so. They would be old now, as I am. Did they seem old? I do not think so."

"Perhaps they are the young of the ones you saw," Twisted Foot suggested.

"That is possible," Old Man Crazy said. "The dead one was young. They have little ones, like the buffalo and antelope. In time there will be many of them. I believe it

[78]

will be so. And the people who have them and are wise enough to use them will become the rulers of the plains. Remember that, little brother, for it is of great importance. No others can stand against them."

"Do you mean that we shall have more than one— many of them?" Twisted Foot cried, astounded by the thought.

"Yes," Old Man Crazy replied. "Kills Something would not listen to me, but I believe it. Horses are come."

Because of his youth and inexperience, Twisted Foot missed the full significance of Old Man Crazy's words. "How are we going to get one, father?" he said. "How will we make it understand the Comanche tongue?"

"We will get one," Old Man Crazy said meditatively. "We will get one, little brother. All Indians will get one."

"All?" Twisted Foot said, puzzled.

"Yes," Old Man Crazy said. "But we must be first. That is important, little brother. The Comanches must have horses first, or they will never come back to the buffalo country."

"I will try, father," Twisted Foot said earnestly. "But I fear they do not know our words."

"We will talk to them," Old Man Crazy said.

Twisted Foot shook his head. "They will not wait to listen."

"We must make them," Old Man Crazy said. "We must find a way to make them listen."

"How?" Twisted Foot asked.

"I have not thought it out yet," Old Man Crazy said. He became silent and a few seconds later he cast a quick look as if daring Twisted Foot to doubt him. "I am thinking on it. Here, let me have your sleeping robe."

Twisted Foot handed over the skin. Old Man Crazy took his worn stone knife from his belt, trimmed off the irregular portions of the hide and then began to cut a wide strong strip of leather from it, working around and around the edge.

"Why do you do that, father?" Twisted Foot asked, curious and also somewhat vexed.

"I will make a rope," Old Man Crazy said. "Since your tongue cannot be still, go and get some meat. We will be here for a length of time. Be certain to bring also the hide."

CHAPTER SEVEN

IT WAS MIDMORNING of a day bright, still, and becoming warm on the prairie. The four horses had been grazing leisurely since shortly after daylight and now they left the grass and went in single file toward the trees, the brown stallion in the lead. The gray mare walked behind him, and the black mare behind her. The young stallion was at the rear, following his mother. He was aware that a dislike of him was forming in the older stallion, a dislike born of jealousy. He did not entirely understand this yet, but he knew the meaning of bared teeth and flattened ears and he kept his distance from the older horse. This enmity did not completely dampen his young and exuberant spirits, however, and he lagged behind and kept raising his dark head to look about for something unusual or exciting, any excuse to kick up his heels and charge, snorting, after the others. No excuse offered, so presently he took a turn over the grass just for the sheer pleasure of it, before following his mother into the trees.

The brown stallion was first at the stream. He was a wiry animal, with a deep powerful chest and strong legs.

His head was straight-lined, tapering to a fine muzzle with wide nostrils. The two mares came up while he was drinking and plunged in their noses. The young stallion waited until the others had left the water before he drank.

In the pleasant shade, the horses settled themselves into positions of rest. Their heads lowered and their lids drooped over drowsy eyes; their ears and tails relaxed. Soon only the soft droning of the insects, also enjoying the shade, could be heard.

"Horses, we have come—" The voice, cracked and hoarse but striving to sound calming, spoke in the Comanche language. Old Man Crazy had intended to add: "to teach you the words of the Comanche tongue." But he did not have time.

It was as if the opening had suddenly shrieked a danger warning. The four horses jerked into quick life. The brown stallion gave forth a blasting snort. The next instant, with a dirt-throwing drive of hoofs, they tore through the screening brush in the direction of the prairie. In seconds they were gone, only the thud of their feet and the shaking bushes telling of their flight.

Old Man Crazy and Twisted Foot, lying in their hiding place under the leaves, looked at each other in keen dismay. Twisted Foot doubted whether it would be wise for him to speak, for this had been Old Man Crazy's plan. Since early morning they had been waiting in the cover.

"Something scared them," Old Man Crazy observed thoughtfully after a time.

"Yes," Twisted Foot agreed gently.

Old Man Crazy shook his head in a slightly bewildered manner. "The tongue is strange to them," he said. "They do not understand Comanche."

"No," Twisted Foot said.

There was a silence of several minutes, then Old Man Crazy said, "Did I not tell you there was nothing to fear, that they would not attack us?"

"Yes, father, you told me," Twisted Foot said.

"Well, they did not," Old Man Crazy said, nodding his head in happy confirmation of his own wisdom.

"No, they did not," Twisted Foot agreed. "You were right in regard to that, father."

Old Man Crazy pushed up to a sitting position at the edge of the opening and discarded all pretense. "It was not a wise plan," he admitted. "Something was wrong. I had hoped they would stay and listen while we talked to them in Comanche."

"It was too sudden," Twisted Foot gave as his opinion. "It startled them."

"Yes," Old Man Crazy said, nodding his head. He had brought the coil of braided buckskin rope that had been Twisted Foot's sleeping robe and now it was hooked over one of his skinny arms. "It is not the way. I will think of some other way. You will see, little brother. I will find a way to make them listen to us. I will set my thoughts to it."

"Will they come back to this place?" Twisted Foot asked.

Old Man Crazy shrugged. "If you would know that, go and watch them," he said. "Notice how far they run, where they halt and how long their fright lasts."

"I will do that, father," Twisted Foot answered readily, welcoming the opportunity.

Old Man Crazy nodded consent. "I will be at the place where we had our fire. Have care you do not startle them still further." He turned and started down the stream, a small, bony old man with his sleeping robe over one shoulder and the coil of leather on his arm.

When Twisted Foot reached the edge of the trees he saw the horses, well out on the prairie. They had halted and were standing with their heads up, looking back. He stopped, hoping they had not seen him. They stood where they were several seconds, then the brown stallion turned and went on. Immediately the others followed him, their heads and tails up. The stallion kept at a steady trot up a gentle rise, and presently all of them went out of sight over the crest.

Twisted Foot knew a keen discouragement. It seemed hopeless. He felt a lonesomeness for Kill Something's village and the pleasant family life of his father's lodge. He would soon need new moccasins again and at home his mother would make them, knowing just how to fashion the right one round to fit his crippled foot. He would like to see Follows Bees again, for they hunted much together.

It would be a long trip to the ravine country, but he was not afraid. Additional days would be required to find the village, for Kills Something would keep it hidden, as a precaution against possible enemies. But he could not long keep it hidden from Twisted Foot, who knew the ridges and the trails.

The youth wondered if Old Man Crazy would go. He did not want to go without Old Man Crazy, not now. Old Man Crazy might have a puzzled head, and he said and did strange things, and he was often cranky and irritable, but there was a spark burning inside him that had a magnetic force.

Twisted Foot turned wearily back to the prairie. He knew Old Man Crazy would not go. Old Man Crazy was determined to get a horse, and this determination, Twisted Foot knew, had not been shaken even by the disappointment of the morning. Old Man Crazy was like a wolf with its teeth locked in an antelope's throat; he would not turn loose.

Twisted Foot made his way across the plain, in the direction of the crest over which the horses had disappeared. He did not hurry, believing that hurrying would not be of any help. Nor was he particularly cautious. As a result, he was surprised and chagrined when he walked boldly on the crest to find that the horses had stopped and were grazing in plain sight beyond.

His first impulse was to throw himself to the grass, but immediately he knew this would be useless. The stallion had already seen him, was watching him with head raised and alert. And the other horses had seen him too. Twisted Foot was angry with himself for having been so careless and, since there was nothing else to do, he just stood there, expecting any second the horses would turn and flee. But they didn't. They just stood and watched him back. He waited, and still nothing happened. After a time the brown stallion took a few steps in his direction, not many, to be sure, but that he took any was surprising and bewildering to Twisted Foot. And while Twisted Foot was recovering from his surprise, one of the mares put her head down and began to eat.

Twisted Foot shook his head in perplexity. A buffalo would never do that, nor a deer. Antelope had a strong curiosity that might cause them to stop and gaze at a hunter, but they rarely relaxed enough to graze at such a time. But now two of the horses were eating, with Twisted Foot in open view. He found this difficult to believe, but he could not doubt it. He became tired of standing and sat down, in which position he knew he was not so easily visible, and at once the horses became more nervous and concerned. He stood up again and the horses seemed reassured.

Twisted Foot remained on the crest until dark, watching the horses and wondering about their strange actions. At the last light they were still there, all of them feeding but the young stallion, which seemed more concerned and nervous than the others.

The young Comanche made his way back to the stream through the dark. Old Man Crazy had a small fire going, with several strips of antelope meat cooking above it. "Did you see them, little brother?" he asked, glancing up.

Twisted Foot noticed that Old Man Crazy was sitting in the midst of a litter of buckskin trimmings and was twisting straps of buckskin together, working more by the feel of his fingers than the fire's dim light.

"Yes, father," Twisted Foot said. "They stopped in the grass."

"Did they run a long distance?"

Twisted Foot shook his head. "Only over the first crest."

"Were they still scared?" Old Man Crazy asked.

"I do not know," Twisted Foot said. "I could not tell." Then, somewhat shamefully, he made a confession. "They saw me, father."

"Saw you?" Old Man Crazy repeated unhappily. "Did you lose your senses?"

"I was not careful," Twisted Foot admitted. "I did not intend it, but it happened."

"Now they will leave," Old Man Crazy cried bitterly. "I have made a fine rope, a wonderful rope. Now we will have no opportunity. Why were you so careless?"

Twisted Foot did not reply. He had been thinking about his father's lodge and the warm companionship of Kill Something's village, but there was no excuse for carelessness among Comanche hunters and warriors. He was still more ashamed when he noticed that to make the rope, Old Man Crazy had cut up his own sleeping robe also.

"In which direction did they flee?" Old Man Crazy asked, still angry, his eye catching a red glint from the fire.

"They did not flee," Twisted Foot said. "It is strange, father. I do not understand it. I know they saw me, but they did not flee."

"Did not flee?" Old Man Crazy said, puzzled. "What did they do, if they did not flee?"

"They stood and looked at me," Twisted Foot said.

"And they could see you were a man?" Old Man Crazy said, shaking his head. "This is indeed strange. They fled in great flight from the sound of my voice, yet they did not run from the sight of you." His dark weathered forehead wrinkled in sober thought.

"I do not believe they are of the same nature as the buffalo and deer," Twisted Foot said.

"They are animals," Old Man Crazy contended crossly. "They have four legs, and hair on their bodies. They eat grass and drink water. An arrow will kill one."

Twisted Foot considered this and nodded slowly. "But their heads are different," he said. "They are not only different outside, as we can see, but different in what goes on inside also. When I squatted down and they could not see me, they were more afraid than when they could see me clearly. Is that not strange, father?"

"I do not understand it," Old Man Crazy said, shaking his head again. "How near to them were you?"

[89]

"The flight of four arrows," Twisted Foot said. "After they saw me, I did not know what to do. They looked at me and were nervous, but they did not flee. Later some of them ate grass. They are calmer and not as foolish as the buffalo."

Old Man Crazy was slow in replying. "Yes," he agreed presently. "That must be true. I do not believe buffalo could learn the language of men, not even that of the men with the white skins. The hair on their skulls is too thick and their eyes see only the ground that is immediately before them. Horses are different, but I do not understand how they are different."

"We must learn that," Twisted Foot said soberly. "We must learn the nature of horses, just as we know the nature of the buffalo and antelope. We must learn their nature if we would have one carry burdens for us."

"How can we learn?" Old Man Crazy said. "They flee at the sound of our voices, but they stand and watch when they cannot hear us."

"There is a way," Twisted Foot answered stoutly. "The men with the white skins have proved it."

CHAPTER EIGHT

THE FOLLOWING morning Twisted Foot and Old Man Crazy returned to the clearing in the trees beside the still pool. They secreted themselves in the brush and waited. Near midday, Old Man Crazy said, "They are not coming." His voice was bitter with disappointment.

"No," Twisted Foot said in agreement.

"We scared them away," Old Man Crazy said. "They have left this place."

Twisted Foot considered this, hoping it was not true. "Let us look on the prairie," he suggested.

Old Man Crazy nodded and got to his feet. A small band of antelope could be seen on a distant crest, but nothing else. Twisted Foot looked carefully. "Let us go over that rise," he said presently. "That is where I saw them yesterday."

They trudged across the grass. "Have care," Old Man Crazy warned as they neared the top.

Twisted Foot hesitated, then dropped to his hands and knees and crawled forward. He looked into the swale beyond, then stood up. "They are not here," he said, shaking his head unhappily. "This is where they were."

"Are you sure?" Old Man Crazy asked, coming up.

Twisted Foot nodded. "Come. I will take you to the tracks."

They went on into the swale, to a place where Twisted Foot pointed to indisputable sign. There were hoof prints, droppings and clipped grass. Old Man Crazy looked at this and said, "Find the going-away trail. We will follow them."

Twisted Foot scouted over the swale until he found a single-file trail. He called to Old Man Crazy and they followed it. It led them out of the shallow depression and to a crest, and it held to this crest for some distance.

"When was it made?" Old Man Crazy asked.

"Early this morning, while the grass was still a little wet," Twisted Foot said. Now the grass was dry, for there was a strong sun and its rays were hot on their dark shoulders. Old Man Crazy squinted querulously about with his single eye.

The tracks turned to the left, back toward the stream. Twisted Foot followed them. At the top of a rise he could see the green trees, but there were no horses on the plain. He moved on and a short time later halted suddenly. "There they are, just coming from the trees," he said, with repressed excitement in his voice.

"Down!" Old Man Crazy cried, throwing himself forward to the grass. "Get down, little brother."

Twisted Foot did not get down. "I believe it is a mis-

[92]

take to hide," he said. "How can they come to know us if they cannot see us, father?"

"They will run away," Old Man Crazy said indignantly.

"I do not believe they will," Twisted Foot said. "We will know. Look, already they have seen us."

The horses, though still distant, had their heads up. Twisted Foot recognized the brown stallion as the one in front by his color and by the white spot in his forehead.

Old Man Crazy rose to his knees. "Do they run yet?" he asked.

"No," Twisted Foot said.

"Are you certain they see us?"

"Yes," Twisted Foot told him. "Their heads are up and they look this way."

Old Man Crazy shook his head. "It is strange," he said.

Twisted Foot watched the horses. "Now they move," he said presently.

"Which way? Where do they go?" Old Man Crazy asked quickly.

"This way," Twisted Foot said. "They are walking, coming on to the grass. Now one has its head down and is eating. They are not greatly scared, father."

"It is very strange," Old Man Crazy said again.

A short time later, Twisted Foot said, "Now all of them are eating."

"Perhaps they would come to a flag, like the antelope," Old Man Crazy said. "We could try."

Twisted Foot agreed and tied his piece of white buckskin to the end of his bow. They sat down and Twisted Foot held the flag above their heads. At once the brown stallion raised his head, and the other horses raised theirs.

"They are more nervous," Twisted Foot told Old Man Crazy.

"Have they started to run yet?"

"No," Twisted Foot said, knowing that Old Man Crazy was thinking of the antelopes' habit of running in circles before approaching a flag.

The horses watched the flag, but there was suspicion in their manner rather than curiosity. The stallion became still more nervous and after a time started to move away.

"They will not come to a flag," Twisted Foot said. "They are wiser than antelope."

"I do not understand it," Old Man Crazy said, shaking his head.

Twisted Foot stood up and untied the piece of buckskin. The horses noticed the movement but it did not excite them.

Old Man Crazy asked, "What will we do now? We have found them and they do not run, but neither can we get them to come to us."

Twisted Foot said, "Perhaps we can go to them. We will try."

"It would be most strange," Old Man Crazy said, but he got to his feet and followed.

Twisted Foot walked slowly. The horses immediately stopped eating and raised their heads, and the brown

[94]

stallion showed new signs of nervousness. The young black stallion ran a few steps. Twisted Foot halted.

"What is it?" Old Man Crazy asked. "Do they run?"

"No, but they watch," Twisted Foot answered. "We will wait here."

The horses continued watching the two Indians. Many slow minutes passed before they put their heads down again. Twisted Foot started walking. The horses raised their heads. Twisted Foot stopped.

"What happens?" Old Man Crazy asked anxiously.

"They are nervous," Twisted Foot said.

But the horses did not run, and after a time all but the young black resumed feeding. Twisted Foot took a few steps, then halted. Next he moved at an angle, not going directly toward the horses.

"Do they run yet?" Old Man Crazy wanted to know.

"No," Twisted Foot said, whispering.

"How far are they?" Old Man Crazy asked, also whispering.

"Three arrow flights," Twisted Foot said.

"And they see us?" Old Man Crazy asked.

"Yes, there is no doubt of it, father," Twisted Foot said.

Old Man Crazy shook his head, unable to understand it.

Twisted Foot started walking again, took several steps, and halted. He took several more, watching the horses closely. He stopped.

"What is it now?" Old Man Crazy whispered.

"They move away," Twisted Foot said.

"Do they run?" Old Man Crazy asked.

"No. They walk," Twisted Foot told him. "They do not appear to be greatly scared, but they do not want us to come any nearer. Now they have stopped. They watch us."

Some time passed and Twisted Foot said, "I will try now." He started walking again, but took only a few steps before halting.

"They will not let us approach them?" Old Man Crazy guessed.

"No," Twisted Foot said. "When I walk, they walk. But I am nearer now than before. I will try again."

He started walking and halted almost immediately, and because of the noise of the hoofs, Old Man Crazy did not have to be told what was happening. "They run," he said resignedly.

"Yes," Twisted Foot admitted.

"I knew it would happen," Old Man Crazy said. "They have been taught not to like Indians."

"But they were not scared, not like buffalo or deer," Twisted Foot said.

"What difference does it make?" Old Man Crazy said. "We cannot catch them."

"Now they have stopped," Twisted Foot said. "I can still see them. They stand and watch us. They have good eyes, father."

Old Man Crazy was thinking of something else. "A trap," he said presently. "That is what we need—a trap large enough to catch a horse."

Twisted Foot was of course familiar with traps and snares of all kinds, for all Indian youths were carefully trained in the making and use of them. Next to the bow and arrow they were the most important method of securing food, especially the smaller kinds of animals and birds. Given a piece of rawhide string, no Indian went hungry long in brush country. But a trap large enough and strong enough to hold a horse was something Twisted Foot had not thought of before.

"We have no trap, father," he told Old Man Crazy.

"We could make one," Old Man Crazy answered.

"It would need to be a very strong one," Twisted Foot said, shaking his head dubiously.

"Yes," Old Man Crazy said. "I have not thought all about it yet. Come, it is time we went back to our fire."

CHAPTER NINE

"WE COULD DIG a hole, a deep pit with straight walls, and cover it with a layer of slender poles, and cover the poles with a thin covering of earth, and some leaves and grass," Old Man Crazy said, talking as much to himself as to Twisted Foot.

They were back at the side of the stream and had cooked and eaten all of the antelope meat they could comfortably hold. Coals of their fire still winked occasionally in the bed of gray ashes and the stars were many and sparkling in the night overhead. A soft breeze rustled the leaves and spread the warm moist smell of the water. Old Man Crazy lay on the hair side of an antelope hide, his thin dark face up to the sky.

Twisted Foot sat cross-legged near the ashes. "I too have thought of a pit, father," he said, "but I do not have much faith in it."

"Deer and antelope are caught in that manner, even the great bulls of the buffalo," Old Man Crazy reminded him.

"There are many of them. They move everywhere,"

Twisted Foot said. "But the horses are few. Many moons could pass before one of them would walk over a pit."

"We have time," Old Man Crazy said obstinately.

Twisted Foot shook his head and asked, "Where would we put it?" Old Man Crazy did not answer immediately, and Twisted Foot went on, "On the plains? At the side of the stream? There is grass everywhere, and the stream has two sides. Horses are wiser than buffalo, father. We would not catch one."

Old Man Crazy mumbled unhappily a few seconds, then became silent. Twisted Foot thought about the horses they had seen during the day, and tried to think of a way they might catch one. The horses had not seemed afraid, but had watched him and had moved away only when he tried to draw near them. Even if he could get his hands on one, he knew he could not hold it. He would need the rope Old Man Crazy had made, and he was not certain he could do it with a rope. Horses obviously had great strength, and also—a thought which gave him much concern—they had powerful feet and teeth. He remembered how frightened the Ute hunter had been and the deep red scratches on the man's back. Still, Old Man Crazy had seen horses and they did not attack the men with white skins.

"Did the men with the white skins have sticks or clubs to protect themselves with, father?" Twisted Foot asked.

"No," Old Man Crazy said. "Some of them had the long sticks that spoke with a loud voice and made much smoke. And some of them had long knives that gleamed."

"Did they use these against the horses?"

"No," Old Man Crazy said, "I do not believe it. Once I saw one strike the horse with a small stick, the size of an arrow's shaft, but it was not in fear. The horse moved very quickly. It was clear that it had a regard for the stick."

"Could the men with the white skins hold the horses by the ropes about their necks?" Twisted Foot asked.

"Yes," Old Man Crazy said. "Their necks are not strong against a rope for some reason. Also the men had harnesses of rawhide straps that they put on their heads. They put things in their mouths too, hard things like little round sticks which were held in place by the rawhide straps."

"Why did they do that?" Twisted Foot asked.

"It was to keep their mouths open—or closed, I forget which," Old Man Crazy said. "Some horses would try to bite the Indians. I saw it."

"But not the men with the white skins?" Twisted Foot said. "Is there a difference between our skins and their skins?"

"They seemed the same, except for color," Old Man Crazy said.

"Could it be that the smell is different?" Twisted Foot asked thoughtfully.

"I do not know," Old Man Crazy said. "It could be. Many things I did not understand."

"Perhaps horses do not like any skin except that which is white," Twisted Foot said. "They understand only the tongue of the men with white skins. Perhaps that is the reason they do not let us catch them."

Old Man Crazy considered this for several seconds, then said, "We must not let it stop us, little brother. It is not proven and we must not let it stop us. Our people have a great need for horses."

"It would be pleasing," Twisted Foot agreed.

Old Man Crazy shook his head half angrily. "Why is it you do not hear me, little brother? Is it that already you are deaf, like Kills Something and the others?"

"But I hear you, father," Twisted Foot said, his eyes perplexed. Sometimes there was simply no understanding of Old Man Crazy. "And Kills Something is not deaf."

"Every one is deaf . . . and blind," Old Man Crazy said bitterly. Then, to make his meaning still more confusing to Twisted Foot, he added, "But me. And I am old and weak. It is a burden which the spirits should not have put on one so feeble."

Now, the spirits having been brought into the conversation, Twisted Foot knew that to try to understand was useless, so he merely said, "Yes, father."

"But I will do it," Old Man Crazy declared defiantly. "In the morning we will make a snare. I have made a fine rope, and in the morning we will make a snare. I will make you see, little brother."

Twisted Foot had made many snares, snares of rawhide

thongs or twisted sinew, and had caught many animals in them, but mostly rabbits and prairie dogs and an occasional fox or badger. Sometimes he had caught ground-running birds, such as speckled quail and the prairie grouse. Once he had caught a big lynx, but it had fought its way free. He had heard the older men talk of snaring deer in the country of many trees and he knew this had failed more often then it was successful.

"It will have to be a big snare, father," he said.

"Yes," Old Man Crazy agreed.

"And a very strong one," Twisted Foot said.

"Do you think I do not know that?" Old Man Crazy retorted sharply. "Now I will sleep."

When morning came, and after a breakfast of meat, Old Man Crazy took up the rope he had made. He was proud of this rope and insisted on carrying it himself. He led the way up the stream to the small opening, where they had first seen the horses. He approached cautiously and asked, "Are they near, little brother?"

"No," Twisted Foot told him, after a careful look around.

Old Man Crazy went into the opening, stood in the center, and studied it with his one eye. The trees were smaller and the brush was heavier on the side toward the plain, and through this brush there was a kind of natural trail, more open than the rest. After a time Old Man Crazy moved to this trail, knelt and felt of the tracks in the soil. "They have passed this way often," he said. "We will put the snare here. Find a long limber stick."

Twisted Foot searched among the bushes and secured a suitable limb. When he returned, Old Man Crazy had fashioned a big loop in the end of the rope. Old Man Crazy took the limb, bent it into a circle and, with small strings of hide, tied the loop to the circle. He looked about until he found a tree with a strong overhanging limb. "Climb up and tie the rope, little brother," he directed. "Tie it so it cannot slip."

Twisted Foot climbed the tree and crawled out on the gnarled branch. While Old Man Crazy directed from below, he wrapped the rope about the branch and fastened it firmly. Back on the ground, he saw that the loop, held in a wide circle by the bent limb, was suspended about four feet above the center of the trail. Old Man Crazy took additional leather strings and, from bushes on either side, anchored the loop firmly in place. Then he carefully arranged the bushes in a manner to disguise the outline of the circle. "There," he said presently. "Is it not a good snare, little brother?"

"Yes," Twisted Foot said. "A startled deer would be caught. But will a horse?"

"Is a horse any different?" Old Man Crazy demanded, half angry. "It has a head, and a neck."

Twisted Foot did not answer, knowing that arguing was useless when Old Man Crazy was in this mood.

"We need meat," Old Man Crazy said presently. "Have care not to frighten the horses so they will not come back to this place."

Twisted Foot took up his bow and left the trees. At the

fringe he looked carefully into the plain. He could not see the horses and believed, because of where he had seen them the afternoon before, they were somewhere to his left. Therefore he turned to the right and made his way into the grass. He walked for several miles before he caught sight of an antelope. He approached as close as he thought wise, then lay down and put up his flag. Considerable time passed before the herd came close enough for a shot. He killed a fat young buck with a single arrow.

Old Man Crazy was not at the camp. Twisted Foot hung the meat from a convenient limb and made a fire. When there was a good bed of coals, he suspended a piece of meat above it. Later he retied the meat so that the side that had been up was now down, thus causing it to roast evenly.

Shortly before the shadows became dense under the trees Old Man Crazy arrived, peering from side to side with little birdlike movements of his head. He sniffed with satisfaction at the smell of the cooking meat. "It is good, little brother. I would eat," he said.

Twisted Foot put meat on a piece of flat bark and Old Man Crazy immediately bit off a piece, hot and dripping with juice. No attempt was made at talking until they had finished eating. Old Man Crazy stretched back on the green antelope hide with a grunt of contentment. "Did you see the horses, little brother?" he asked.

"No," Twisted Foot said.

Old Man Crazy mused a bit, then said, "I hope they have not left this place."

Twisted Foot knew then that Old Man Crazy had not seen them either. "They were not greatly scared," he said. "They did not run but only walked away."

"They are still here," Old Man Crazy said. "They will come back to the opening. There is no other as good along the stream. We will catch one. And after we get one, we can catch others. You will see, little brother."

In spite of his wishes, Twisted Foot could not feel so sure. The horses were big and strong, and not fools. "Do you believe we can teach it the Comanche words, and to like us, father?" he asked soberly.

"Yes," Old Man Crazy said. "We will teach it. It shall know the Comanche tongue as well as it knows that of the men with the white skins. We will go early to the opening in the morning, little brother."

The sun still slanted sharply through the trees when they arrived. They approached cautiously, eager for the first glimpse of the snare. It was unsprung, empty. The opening was also empty.

"There is nothing, father," Twisted Foot said. He could not keep the disappointment out of his voice.

"Look at the ground," Old Man Crazy said. "Have they been here since yesterday?"

Twisted Foot went to the trail. "No," he said. "They did not come."

"Then it is not the fault of the snare," Old Man Crazy said. "We will wait. They will come. You will see, little brother."

But the horses did not come, not that day. Late in the

afternoon Twisted Foot suggested going into the grass, to see if they could find them. Old Man Crazy shook his head. "They will come," he declared. "This is one of their places to drink and rest."

Twisted Foot could not help being doubtful and restless, but he stayed with Old Man Crazy. At dark they went back to their camp and cooked a good meal of antelope meat. The next morning they returned to the opening. The snare was as they had left it, hardly noticeable even to their knowing eyes in its setting of bushes but unsprung.

"I will go and see where they are," Twisted Foot suggested hopefully.

Old Man Crazy shook his head and said, "This is where we will catch one, little brother."

And that day, shortly after the sun had reached its position of strongest warmth, they did come. Twisted Foot first caught a view of them through the trees. "They come, father," he whispered excitedly. "They are coming."

"Get down. Hide," Old Man Crazy ordered sharply, and they scuttled to positions already selected in the brush.

The horses came steadily across the grass in single file, the brown stallion in the lead. The gray mare was next, and behind her was the black mare. The black colt loafed along indifferently in the rear, pausing now and then to take tempting bites of grass.

They came directly to the trees and the brown stallion entered the natural aisle. Twisted Foot felt the breath grow tight in his chest, like a hard lump beneath him. The horse came on toward the loop, walking in an easy unhurried manner. He halted, lifted his head slightly and pointed his ears forward toward the opening. The gray stopped behind him, and the black mare beyond her. The black mare turned her head to look at the young stallion, which had not yet entered the trees.

They stood there like that for what seemed to Twisted Foot to be a long time. The stallion sniffed the warm motionless air, and the young stallion came and halted behind the black mare. Finally the brown started on. He came to within a few feet of the snare. His head was almost in it and Twisted Foot did not dare take his eyes from the scene. Then the horse stopped again.

The upper part of the loop was above the stallion's head and he did not seem to notice it. But the lower part was chest-high across the trail. It could have been just another limb, easy to brush aside, though Twisted Foot knew that pressure would break the strings, permitting the loop to collapse about the horse's neck.

The stallion stood there a long minute, not appearing to notice the loop or in any way be excited. Then he casually turned through the brush to one side and went around it. The other horses, coming behind him, followed exactly in his tracks, all avoiding the snare.

Twisted Foot let the air escape from his lungs in a soft

sigh of disappointment. He turned to look at Old Man Crazy and found the old Indian still and intent. Old Man Crazy's fingers closed on his arm in a signal to be silent.

The horses entered the opening and the stallion went to the stream. He glanced about before plunging his nose into the water. The two mares pushed up beside him and drank. The young stallion held back until the others had finished and as he went forward, the older stallion, leaving the water, suddenly backed his ears and struck out with his teeth in a quick and ill-tempered movement. The young black was not caught unawares. He leaped swiftly aside, clearing the old stallion's path. The old stallion's anger seemed to pass as abruptly as it had come, for he did not pursue but moved on to a resting place in the shade. The young stallion went to the water and drank. Twisted Foot noted with some concern the brown horse's temper and quickness and remembered the Ute hunter's story of having been attacked. Now it was not difficult to believe.

The two Indians lay still and silent in their hiding place. The horses found positions to their liking in the shade and drowsed. The gray mare lay down and rolled, flinging her hoofs into the air. She got up, shook herself and moved to a place near the black mare. The young stallion took a position at a distance from the older stallion.

Time passed, slow, warm and drowsy. Twisted Foot wondered what they, he and Old Man Crazy, would do next. It was apparent that the snare they had made was not going to be successful. The horses knew it was there. Twisted Foot doubted that any snare would be successful. Horses were too deliberate and knowing in their movements. They did not run foolishly along a path like a rabbit or a ground squirrel, or blunder about indifferently like a badger. They were wise, unquestionably wiser than the other animals Twisted Foot knew . . .

There was a sudden movement beside him, and he felt rather than saw Old Man Crazy pop up out of the brush. The horses started to quick alertness. Old Man Crazy gave a wild yell, causing Twisted Foot to believe that the old Indian had really lost his mind. The four horses whirled and in single jumps were headed for the open. Then Twisted Foot knew Old Man Crazy had not lost his mind. This was the way, if there was a way, to put a horse in the snare, for in their fright they would not be so deliberate. The brown stallion, in the lead, took the natural opening. He was going at full speed when he came to the snare and he did not shorten his stride in the least.

The strings snapped, the bent limb leaped free and straight, and the loop in the rope spun about the stallion's neck. The bushes and branches heaved as if suddenly hit by a mighty wind and the tree itself swayed and swung, and there was a cracking and crashing that almost froze Twisted Foot in his hiding place. Old Man Crazy went hopping forward. Twisted Foot leaped up and ran after him.

The gray mare had been hard on the stallion's heels through the natural opening. She bounced against him and both went down. The black mare tore through the brush at the right, making her own opening. The young black ran under the trees for a distance before turning through the undergrowth.

The tree to which the rope was attached jerked spasmodically as Old Man Crazy and Twisted Foot hurried forward. Twisted Foot could hardly believe it was true, that they had actually caught a horse.

Both horses were up. The gray mare was racing on toward the prairie, and the stallion had whirled and was facing them. His head was up and his big eyes flashed fire. Twisted Foot and Old Man Crazy halted, frightened and not knowing what to do. The stallion turned back to the plain and charged forward. The loop had tightened well down on his neck, giving him all the advantage of the great strength of his shoulders. He flung himself violently against the rope. The tree bent, leaned and creaked, but it held. The strain, however, was too much for the limb. It broke at a weakened knot near the rope. The stallion fell forward, quickly regained his feet and went galloping on, out into the grass, neighing wildly to the other horses. Behind him trailed Old Man Crazy's carefully plaited rope, with the piece of limb bouncing crazily at its end. Forgetting the other horses, the stallion raced across the prairie in frantic flight.

CHAPTER TEN

FOR A LONG moment after the brown stallion had galloped away, neither Twisted Foot nor Old Man Crazy spoke. So violent had been the horse's struggles that Twisted Foot had actually known a sense of relief when the limb parted. But immediately he became depressed and disappointed. He felt that there was nothing left for him and Old Man Crazy now but to go to the ravine country and search for Kills Something's village. He did not see how they could catch one of the horses, and he was far from certain as to what they would do with one if they did catch it. Not until now had he fully realized their great strength. He wondered soberly if the task was not simply too much for him and Old Man Crazy. They needed his father and the other men of the village to help them.

"He was very strong," Old Man Crazy said slowly, still blinking his eye.

"Yes," Twisted Foot said. "I do not know how we could hold him, father. Almost he pulled up the tree."

"It was a good rope," Old Man Crazy said.

"He was greatly scared," Twisted Foot said.

"If he had not been scared, he would not have entered the snare," Old Man Crazy replied.

"That is true," Twisted Foot agreed.

"But he was very scared," Old Man Crazy said, shaking his head in recollection of the violent struggle. "I could hardly believe it."

"It was the limb that broke," Twisted Foot said. "It was not that I tied the rope badly."

"It was a fine rope. The rope did not break," Old Man Crazy said.

"We can make another one," Twisted Foot said.

"Not as good as that one," Old Man Crazy said sadly. "We have only fresh hides and not many of them. It was the finest rope I ever made."

"It is gone now," Twisted Foot said regretfully. "The horse carried it away."

"We can get it back," Old Man Crazy said, his eye brightening with a sudden thought. "You can get it back, little brother."

Twisted Foot was surprised. "How is that possible?" he asked.

"You have but to follow the stallion's trail," Old Man Crazy told him. "The rope is loose on his neck. It will drop off when he puts his head down to eat or to drink. It will not be difficult, little brother. You will find it somewhere by his trail. We will make another snare, one that will not fail. I know how it can be done. But it is necessary for us to have the rope."

Twisted Foot hesitated. "Are you certain it will drop off?" he asked.

"Yes," Old Man Crazy said. "Think on it and you yourself will know that it must be. But you will have to follow the trail closely, for the rope may be at any place along it. It will fall off when his head is down."

"I will follow it," Twisted Foot said. He turned back to the bushes and took up his bow and quiver of arrows.

Old Man Crazy nodded strong approval and said, "Follow until you get the rope, little brother. I will wait at the camp."

Twisted Foot struck out across the plain. No horses could be seen but the trail of the stallion was easy to follow, because of the dragging limb and because the horse had been running in great leaps. Twisted Foot increased his pace to a trot, uneven because of his crippled foot. The trail led straight. At the first crest Twisted Foot slowed to a cautious walk, but the horse was not in the swale beyond. A short distance beyond the crest, however, Twisted Foot found the piece of limb, where it had bounced free of the rope. He looked about, thinking that the rope might be there too, but it wasn't.

In the swale the trail became more difficult and Twisted Foot knew the stallion had slowed his gait. Twisted Foot was forced to go slower also, and in places all of his skill was necessary to follow the sign over the grass. Twice he got down on his hands and knees and felt his way along hoof prints that could not be seen.

He saw a rabbit, squatted with flattened ears in a shallow form. Normally he would have paid no attention to it, but now he shot it and tied it to his belt. The sun went down a short time later. Twisted Foot straightened and searched the country in the last light. He saw several antelope, and two gray wolves stalking them, and an eagle wheeling high on motionless wings. He saw the mounds of a prairie dog colony, a gray badger waddling among them in search of a meal. On a distant crest there were several larger animals which he recognized by color and shape as buffalo. But nowhere were there any horses, the brown stallion or others.

Twisted Foot gathered buffalo chips and made a small fire. He skinned the rabbit and cut it into pieces. He stuck two pieces on sticks and held them over the little blaze. He had plenty of time so he let them cook thoroughly, and the meat was tender and juicy. Finishing the rabbit, he pulled grass for his bed and was asleep before the stars had all twinkled into view overhead.

He awoke while the sky was all silvered the next morning and took the trail as soon as it was light enough to see. His belly was flat and empty, but that did not worry him. A lean stomach travels with less effort than a full one.

The trail showed that the stallion had quit running and had been walking and grazing. Twisted Foot searched all the turns and wanderings, watching carefully for the rope, but he did not find it. About midmorning, however, he saw the horse, a distant brown object standing on a grassy knoll. It was too far to tell whether the rope was still about the animal's neck, so Twisted Foot kept to the sign. The trail led him nearer and nearer the horse, and presently he saw that the animal had discovered him, for its head was up and it was looking in his direction. Twisted Foot thought, but was not sure, that he could see a thin line curving downward from the horse's neck. He dared not quit the sign, however, until he was certain, for if the rope had dropped off and he once passed it, there was little likelihood of his ever finding it. He remembered Old Man Crazy's anxiousness to recover it, though he doubted that the old Indian had expected the task to be so difficult.

Twisted Foot watched the stallion as he followed the trail, and after a time the horse showed indications of nervousness and started away. He walked with his head held curiously to one side, and after studying him for several seconds, Twisted Foot realized the reason. The stallion was still dragging the rope and walked with his head to one side to keep the rope from under his feet, thus avoiding the jerks that would result when he stepped on it.

The youth halted, knowing there was no point any longer in carefully following the trail. He knew now where the rope was, but how could he get it? He couldn't, not until it fell off. And when would it do that? There was

[116]

no way of telling. Perhaps at a time when the animal had its head down feeding, or even more likely when it drank, for then it would have lowered its head as far as possible to reach the water. Twisted Foot remembered how the horses had drunk at the stream and it seemed certain that the loop, if it were not snug, would then slip off. At the same time he realized that if it were tight, it might never come off.

Twisted Foot had an impulse to return to the stream and tell Old Man Crazy that it was useless to try to regain the rope. It would be easier and certainly quicker to make another rope, even though they had no cured hides. Still, with the rope in sight, he was reluctant to give up. There was the rope, and there was the horse, each as unobtainable as the other. Twisted Foot tried to think of the best thing for him to do.

The horse had halted and was watching Twisted Foot. He did not appear excited or anxious to leave, but when Twisted Foot started, he started. And when Twisted Foot stopped, the horse stopped. Twisted Foot realized that he was gaining nothing and moreover, as long as the horse had its head up or was moving, there was no chance that the rope might slip off. He wished the horse would graze, but it kept watching him.

Twisted Foot saw a movement in the grass. It was a flock of prairie chickens. They reminded him that he was hungry. Too, he liked the big white-meated birds and did not often get an opportunity for one. Putting an arrow in his bow, he stalked the prairie chickens and shot one. The others took wing. Twisted Foot looked at the horse, wondering if all this had frightened it. The horse was still where it had been, still watching him in a mildly indifferent manner. Twisted Foot had intended to carry the bird until a more convenient time to eat it, but there seemed nothing else to do then, so he skinned it and made a fire. While he was eating, he saw the horse lower its head and begin eating. This pleased him, for it was what he wanted. Now perhaps the rope would fall off. He sat and watched, the sun beating down on his lean dark back.

The horse grazed for some time, then lifted his head and started away, and by the manner in which the horse carried his head to one side Twisted Foot knew the rope was still about his neck. He sat there another minute or two, considering whether to return to Old Man Crazy, then he pushed erect, slung his arrow quiver on his back and trudged on after the horse. At least now, as long as he kept the horse in sight, he did not have to puzzle out the faint trail. Also, judging from his own thirst, he believed that it was about time the stallion went to water.

They moved across the wide prairie under the glare of the sun, head-down stallion in front and limping Indian youth behind. For an hour they kept this pace, neither excited and neither hurrying. Sometimes the horse disappeared over a rise, but when Twisted Foot later topped it, the stallion was still in front, still moving steadily.

Twisted Foot expected the horse to circle back to the

left, toward the stream and water, but the horse kept going in a straight direction, over one rise after another and through the swales. Twisted Foot began to wish seriously for water, for he had not drunk since the previous day, but he kept on. The stallion had not drunk since the previous day either.

Long dry miles passed beneath their feet. The stallion kept moving, still holding his head to one side. He knew of course that Twisted Foot was behind him, but this no longer seemed to be of any concern. And Twisted Foot was thinking more and more about water. How long, he wondered, could a horse go without drinking? Was he like the little pocket-mouse that lived in the grass and never had to go to water? Was the horse trying to get rid of him by thirst? No. Horses could not be that smart and he knew they drank, and copiously, for he and Old Man Crazy had seen them.

They were miles from the stream, but the stallion kept moving with a purpose and Twisted Foot kept telling himself that it had to be water. The horse must know where it was going. And he, Twisted Foot, could not go another night without water. It became a question of whether to cut across the prairie for known water or trust the horse. Twisted Foot considered it for several minutes, his mouth so dry his tongue was beginning to thicken. Presently he decided to stick with the horse.

It was late in the afternoon before Twisted Foot knew he had been right. In a swale there was a clump of trees, surrounded by brush so luxuriantly green it could mean only one thing—a water hole.

The stallion quickened his stride. Twisted Foot did too, indifferent now to the effect on the horse. Reaching the brush, the stallion went in without hesitation and was still there when Twisted Foot arrived. The young Indian paused only long enough for a glance around. It was a little shallow lake, shrunken by the summer heat and lack of rain. The stallion stood at its edge, water draining back from his lifted muzzle. Twisted Foot noticed only that the rope had not fallen off before he pushed on to the water himself. The stallion moved on, around the lake shore. Twisted Foot threw himself flat and drank. He raised his head, then drank some more, filling his body with the warm liquid. Presently he pushed back on his haunches and turned to look at the horse, and was somewhat surprised to find that it was less than an arrow's distance away, though across the water, and was regarding him without any apparent fright.

A sudden realization came to Twisted Foot, one that caused his pulse to quicken. He could get the rope now. At that distance he could drive one of his stone-pointed arrows into a vital spot, behind the foreleg or even into the neck, and the rope would be his. He remembered how anxious Old Man Crazy was to recover the rope, and there were other horses—the two mares and the young black stallion. Living by the arrow, he was accustomed to killing when he needed food. But some inner instinct rebelled against it now. A horse was somehow different, and this particular one, so well-known from watching and following, was beginning to be like an old friend.

Twisted Food pushed the thought from his mind and immediately something else took its place. It was nearing the time of the day when Twisted Foot was accustomed to eating and he was hungry, despite the grouse. He picked up his bow and moved back from the water, into the brush, knowing enough of the nature of the country to be confident he would not have to wait long. The stallion moved on farther around the lake and began nibbling at the grass.

Not many minutes passed before a young wolf came trotting across the prairie. Twisted Foot watched it, knowing from the bulge of its stomach it had eaten only recently. Nearing the brush, the wolf slowed and sniffed the air in natural caution. The wind was wrong for him to receive Twisted Foot's scent and he moved on in and went to water. The Indian youth could have killed him as he drank, but he didn't, for the Comanches believed the wolves were in some manner connected with the guardian spirits.

The wolf finished drinking and left, and not long afterwards a big bobcat, with a short ringed tail and black tufted ears, emerged from a thicket and made its way on padded paws to the water's edge. Twisted Foot's arrow struck it full in the side as it put its head down to drink. The Comanches had no aversion to bobcat meat. Also

Twisted Foot was pleased to have the thick furry skin. It would be soft under his hips and shoulders to sleep on.

In the growing darkness, the youth made a fire and roasted a side of bobcat ribs. He ate until he was contented, then spread the hide in a spot protected on three sides by heavy brush, for he knew that animals would be coming and going to the water during the night. He heard them later, antelope and deer, and once perhaps, from their heavy grunting, some buffalo, and he knew there were many others of the soft-footed kind, such as rabbits and foxes and badgers, that he did not hear. Flesh side to the ground, the bobcat skin made a good bed.

CHAPTER ELEVEN

WHEN MORNING came, the stallion was gone. Twisted Foot was not surprised. He went to the water's edge, drank and washed, splashing water on his face and arms and body. This completed, he made a fire, knowing that he had a long day before him returning to the camp where Old Man Crazy waited. While the fire burned down to coals, he cut a strip of the tender back meat from the bobcat carcass and fastened it to the end of a pole. The business of cooking and eating took some time, but presently he finished. He picked up his bow and the bobcat skin and went to the lake for a final drink, and when he raised his head he got a surprise for there, coming through the brush to the opposite side, was the brown stallion. Plain to be seen about his neck was the rope, its end trailing on the ground.

Twisted Foot rocked back on his lean haunches and watched meditatively. The horse drank, raised his head and looked across the lake. If he saw anything that concerned him, he did not show it. Presently, he turned and moved to a shady spot under some trees. Here he rubbed his neck against a trunk before settling in a relaxed position to doze.

Twisted Foot remained still for some time, thinking. The horse knew he was there, yet did not seem to be scared. It had rubbed its neck in an effort to get rid of the rope, and another effort might be successful, for even at that distance he could see that the loop was not tight. Old Man Crazy had cleverly put an extra knot in it to prevent choking the horse in the event he had been caught while they were away from the snare.

Twisted Foot decided he would stay there a time and see if the rope came off. Since his stomach was full, he had nothing to do but wait, and around the shore a short distance there was an inviting patch of grassy sunshine. The horse twitched his ears forward when Twisted Foot moved and watched while Twisted Foot walked around and seated himself on the grass. Twisted Foot lay back and closed his eyes. He lay there for an hour, until the sun became uncomfortably warm, before sitting up. The stallion was still under the trees, and it was obvious by now that he was paying but little attention to the young Indian.

Twisted Foot went to the water and drank. He took off his worn moccasins and waded in to his knees, then he splashed himself noisily, deliberately inviting the stallion's attention. The horse merely turned his head to watch.

Twisted Foot was surprised but pleased. He wondered

how far this might go. Back on the bank, he put on his moccasins and began walking slowly along the shore, toward the horse. The stallion raised his head and watched. He shifted his balance to all four feet.

"Do not be afraid," Twisted Foot said in a low casual voice, and was shocked an instant later that he had spoken. The words had come before he thought. He had talked to the horse and, unbelievable as it was, his words seemed to have a calming effect. The stallion twitched his ears forward in an interested fashion.

"Do not be afraid," Twisted Foot repeated. "I do not intend to harm you." Could it be possible, he wondered, that this horse understood Comanche words?

There could be no question but that the stallion was listening. However, as Twisted Foot continued to approach, the animal switched his tail nervously.

Twisted Foot halted. "It is the rope I want," he said, keeping his voice low and calm. "You do not like it about your neck. I will take it away. There is no reason to be afraid. I will not hurt you. It is Old Man Crazy's rope and he told me to get it for him." Twisted Foot discovered that he himself was trembling with excitement, and possibly some of the trembling was from fear. He was not certain, but he kept talking to the horse. Presently the animal gave a snort and whirled, and left at a gallop. But he did not go far before he stopped and turned, and Twisted Foot could see that he was not scared, not really.

"Do not run away," Twisted Foot said. "There is no

need. I will not hurt you. I like you. I will be your friend. I will treat you well, like the men with the white skins treat you."

The horse did not go away, but neither did he come back. Twisted Foot continued talking, greatly pleased that the horse was even listening. "I will not hurt you. There is no reason for you to be afraid. I know you have carried the men with white skins on your back. I would like for you to carry me on your back."

The horse was listening, but he was nervous. Twisted Foot felt the tension mounting, approaching the breaking point. He could feel it in himself as well as in the horse. He knew the horse was going to whirl and flee, but before it did so, Twisted Foot turned and went back around the lake. He walked slowly, but inside him excitement was seething. He had talked to the horse and the horse had listened. He looked back to be sure the stallion was actually there.

Twisted Foot sat and watched the horse, marveling at the progress he had made with it, and just when he had been the most discouraged. A strong warmth for the animal grew in his heart. He had an impulse to go back immediately, to talk some more and press his new-found friendship. But some inner instinct warned him to go slowly, to be patient. Presently he stood up and walked about, in plain sight of the horse, but paying no attention to it, being careful not to approach close enough to make it nervous.

Late in the afternoon the stallion left the water hole and made its way through the trees to the grassy reaches beyond. Twisted Foot saw this with some concern. He became restless and lonesome. After a time, he picked up his bow with the intention of following the horse. He went a short distance, hesitated, and then came back. He sensed that this was a critical time in his relationship with the horse and it was important that he have confidence, in himself as well as in the stallion. He gathered dry wood and made a fire, taking his time in order to keep busy. He fixed a piece of meat to roast and watched it, squatting beside the coals. And he knew a keen thrill of triumph and pleasure when, just before dark, the stallion returned to the water hole. It paused to look toward him before it advanced to drink.

"I am still here," Twisted Food said to himself, for the stallion was too far away to hear. "I will not leave. You are not afraid. You are beginning to know I will not hurt you. I will make you know it."

And in the days that followed at that secluded water hole, Twisted Foot went about this task with deliberate intensity, using all of his natural knowledge and understanding of animals. He was patient and easy and quickly became sure of himself. When the horse was near he talked to it, in soft soothing tones. When the horse did not want to be talked to, he let it alone. When it shied away, he did not follow but gave it time to return of its own accord. He made no attempt to catch it, or to grab the end of the trailing rope, which frequently he could have done, for he had long since realized that the stallion was many times stronger than he was and that he could never control it by force. He knew his only hope lay in the development of understanding and a strong mutual faith.

The stallion, on his side, separated now from the other horses, had the desire for companionship and attention that is inherent in all horses. He was not a wild animal, but came from a long line of ancestors who had known close association with their masters on the deserts of Arabia. Men with white skins had brought him to the plains country, had ridden on his back. It was during a terrifying battle with Indians to the south that he and the two mares and the colt and the young stallion had escaped, and the Indians had further added to their terror by pursuing them and trying to kill them with arrows. The colt had been killed by the Ute hunters. All these things, including the snare Old Man Crazy and Twisted Foot had set, had combined to destroy the horses' confidence in men, to make them shy and distrustful. But now Twisted Foot's ease and patience and kindness began to restore the stallion's confidence.

One afternoon the horse approached to a distance of a few feet and stretched his neck to Twisted Foot. Twisted Foot felt a quick misgiving but controlled an impulse to leap back. He remained perfectly still, even when he felt the hot cautious breath on his arm. The stallion sniffed and smelled deeply, not once but several times. Presently he drew back, apparently satisfied.

Twisted Foot relaxed. "It is good," he said to the animal happily. "I like you. I will not hurt you. I want you to like me too. I will treat you well. You shall have plenty of grass and water, and a shelter when the cold winds blow."

Two days later Twisted Foot ventured to put his hand on the stallion's head. The horse did not shy away and Twisted Foot felt the fine thin hair and the bony skull beneath. The horse lowered his head, so that Twisted Foot's fingers were at the base of his ears.

"Why, you want me to scratch you," Twisted Foot said with quick amazement, and he scratched around the ears gently. "You like your ears scratched."

The stallion obviously enjoyed this and when Twisted Foot paused, he nudged him with his dark nose. Twisted Foot scratched some more and, emboldened, presently rubbed the stallion's neck. He rubbed under the loop of the rope, and the stallion pressed against his hand. Twisted Foot considered taking the rope off, but he didn't have that much confidence, not yet. "I will," he told the horse. "I will take it off, but first we must be very sure. You must know that I am your good friend, that I will never harm you."

Later, when finally Twisted Foot turned away, he heard footsteps behind. He looked back to discover that the stallion was following him. "Come on, come on," he said delightedly. "You can come with me to my fire, Likes-Your-Ears-Scratched."

But after a few steps, Likes-His-Ears-Scratched paused.

[129]

"Very well, do as you wish," Twisted Foot told him. "It is time I made a fire." He went on, to the place near the water where he usually made the fires, and when he turned for a stealthy look, the stallion had his head down and was feeding.

Twisted Foot felt a warm inner happiness. He knew he had won, that he had gained the stallion's confidence. Likes-His-Ears-Scratched was no longer afraid of him and, also important, he, Twisted Foot, was no longer afraid of Likes-His-Ears-Scratched. He knew the horse would not harm him. But still he was not confident that he could control it yet. He had to teach it the Comanche words, words that would cause it to stop when he wished, to go and come, and to turn to the right or to the left. This seemed to be the most difficult task of all, for he did not know how to go about it.

On sudden impulse, Twisted Foot stood up and called, "Come. Come to me, Likes-Your-Ears-Scratched."

The horse lifted its head and looked at Twisted Foot.

"Come. Come to me," Twisted Foot repeated. "Come to me and I will scratch your ears."

The horse put its head down and resumed eating.

"You will," Twisted Foot told him. "When I call, you will come. And also the time will be when you will carry me on your back," he added, though in his own mind he knew that time was not near. Or rather, this is what he thought.

CHAPTER TWELVE

Likes-His-Ears-Scratched was gone when Twisted Foot awoke the next morning. This did not concern Twisted Foot. He was confident that the horse would return, not because he believed that Likes-His-Ears-Scratched had developed any particular liking for him, but for the much more logical and simple reason that this was the only water in miles. He had learned enough about horses during the past days to realize that they were governed primarily by their appetites and the needs of their bodies, just as were all other animals, including men. Likes-His-Ears-Scratched would come back for water and to drowse in the shade, and maybe, Twisted Foot hoped happily, to have his ears scratched and his neck rubbed and to listen to Comanche words.

Twisted Foot cooked his breakfast, then took up his bow. He needed meat and this time decided that he would prefer an antelope. He knew antelope would not be difficult to find, for herds of them watered every night at the little lake. As he left the trees he saw the stallion, feeding not far distant. The horse raised his head and looked at

Twisted Foot a few seconds, then resumed feeding. Just then, filling his stomach was his principal interest.

It was a bright morning, rich in earthy smells on a gentle breeze, and Twisted Foot walked steadily. Several times he saw antelope but he did not halt, for it was in the back of his mind that he might find a covey of prairie chickens as well. He did not find any birds, however, and finally halted on a crest somewhat higher than the others. Here he got out his buckskin flag and tied it to the end of a pole he had brought for that purpose. No antelope were in sight just then, so he settled himself comfortably to wait. He drowsed in the sun an hour or more before the drumming of small hooves caused him to roll over on his stomach and watch. The antelope wheeled to a halt a quarter of a mile away, their dark faces turned to the flag. They stood several minutes, looking and stamping their feet, before their nervous excitement and curiosity put them in motion again. They ran with effortless bounds and before long, as Twisted Foot had known they would, came to another halt, this time near the top of the rise. Twisted Foot was watching them idly when his body suddenly tensed and his keen eyes focused on something far beyond them.

It was slight, a kind of stain in the air. Only eyes trained to see everything would have noticed it. Twisted Foot decided it could be dust—or smoke—either of which interested him. A few seconds were enough to tell that it was moving, but not rapidly. He had seen fires in the dry grass before and they could be terrible, roaring across the prairie at great speed, leaving a black, lifeless earth and seared bodies behind. If, on the other hand, it were dust, it meant a concerted movement. Antelope or deer, traveling slow, would not raise it. A herd of buffalo might. But to Twisted Foot it looked more like an Indian village on the march, like the dust stirred by the ends of travois poles dragging behind dogs and the dust kicked up by human feet.

Forgetting the antelope, Twisted Foot watched the low cloud. Smoke would be darker, he decided, and not so uniform, due to the burning of occasional bushes. Fire too, in that wind, would travel faster, speeded eventually by the suction of its own heat. It was dust. And what was causing it? Buffalo? Or the Utes? Or it might be a band of adventurous Comanches, even Kills Something's village come again to the buffalo country.

Twisted Foot stood up. The antelope whirled and raced away, but that was no longer important. Watching a few seconds longer, Twisted Foot jerked the buckskin from the end of the pole and stuffed it into his belt. Then he started across the plain toward the dust, angling in a direction ahead of it. In his way, he was as curious as the antelope.

Near midday, after miles of steady traveling, Twisted Foot was close enough to make out dark objects at the base of the cloud. He kept going and presently came to the conclusion they were buffalo, from their size and shape. They were big animals. Yet something about them was strange. There seemed to be variations in their color. Some were black, as buffalo should be, but others were lighter and one, at least, seemed white. And white buffalo were so rare that a mythical legend existed concerning them among the Indians. The hunter who was successful in slaying one would forever afterwards be favored by the gods, and his village as well, according to the legend.

Twisted Foot, who had not yet killed even one buffalo, had little hope of killing one of the rare albinos. However he would like to see one, for he knew that this had never been permitted even to some of the best of the Comanche hunters. He thought about Likes-His-Ears-Scratched and disliked being away from the horse so long, but Likes-His-Ears-Scratched was likely dozing contentedly in the shade by this time. Also, by traveling fast, Twisted Foot expected to be back at the water hole that night.

Twisted Foot went down a slope, through a swale, and up to the next rise. Here he paused again, studying the dust and the dark objects, and he became still more puzzled. The color variations he had noticed before were even more apparent and something about the shapes was not completely true to buffalo. Also, from time to time in the dust, there was a strange glint, like the sun shining on water, a thing that could not be explained.

The young Indian left this crest and ran on to the next one. Here he was closer. Almost immediately, in the dust, he caught sight of new shapes, familiar shapes but ones he would never have expected among these animals. The shapes looked like men, walking. They were men. And the other shapes, the big ones, were not buffalo as he had thought. They were horses. There could be no doubt about it; Twisted Foot now knew these animals too well to be mistaken. They were horses, and what he had be-lieved to be the humps of buffalo were bundles on the horses' backs. And some of the horses carried men, just as Old Man Crazy had said.

Twisted Foot sank down to the grass, believing what he saw with difficulty. These were horses, and men were with them. And the men were peculiarly dressed. They wore not just breechcloths, but coverings on their legs and arms and bodies, even on their heads. One of them wore something about his chest that shone brightly when the sun struck it at the right angle. They were strange men, unlike any Twisted Foot had ever seen before. Slowly the truth dawned on him. These were not Indians; they were the men with the white skins, the men Old Man Crazy had talked so much about. These were the things of which Old Man Crazy had told and which the men of Kills Something's village had smiled about, not believing. Now Twisted Foot knew it was true, and the knowledge left him weak and breathless.

They were the men with the white skins. Why had they come? What did they want? Twisted Foot felt a sudden apprehension. Were they seeking the brown stal-

lion? Had they come after his horse? He became immediately antagonistic. They could not have Likes-His-Ears-
Scratched, not now.

He was on the point of turning and hurrying back to
the stallion when the column halted. The dust drifted
away and settled to the ground. Twisted Foot waited to
see what the men would do. They gathered in a small clus-
ter and talked, and occasionally one would wave his arms.
They seemed excited about something, though Twisted
Foot could not determine what it was. The horses stood
with drooping heads and presently, with the dust gone,
he could see them clearly. Four were black and four were
reddish-brown, reminding Twisted Foot of Likes-His-
Ears-Scratched. Three others were yellow, almost the
color of the dry grass, and two were gray, like the gray
mare. Two more were white, whiter, he was sure, than
even the buffalo albino.

A number of the horses carried bundles, big and round
and tied with tightly drawn leather ropes. Men had been
on the backs of the others and now that the men were
gone, Twisted Foot could see the strange-looking leather
seats the men had ridden on. There were leather harnesses
on the heads of these horses too. These were the things
Old Man Crazy had told about, but Old Man Crazy had
not been able to tell how they were used. It was something which Twisted Foot felt a great need to know. He
decided to stay and watch.

The men talked for some time. Occasionally one would

[136]

turn and look about, shading his eyes with his hand. Then another would look. After that there would be more talking. Finally, some of the men started walking forward. The others turned back to the horses and got on their backs. Twisted Foot watched this closely, desiring to know just how it was done. He was amazed that it was so easy. The men went to the horses and put their legs over the horses' backs, and then they were up, sitting on the strange seats. The horses, including those with bundles on their backs, moved on after the men who walked.

Twisted Foot followed the procession, entranced and eager to know still more, for this was knowledge that he planned to use himself in connection with Likes-His-Ears-Scratched. But he took care to keep out of sight as he slipped along, for it was in the back of his mind that these men were searching for the brown stallion.

After an hour or so of slow travel, the men with the white skins stopped again, and again they gathered in a little group to talk. This time Twisted Foot was close enough so their voices occasionally carried to him. The words had no meaning for his ears but he soon realized that the men were not contented. Their tones were loud and quarrelsome. Again at intervals they searched the horizons with their eyes. Twisted Foot wondered if their meat was gone and they were looking for antelope or buffalo.

Presently the men scattered. Several went to the horses with bundles and began taking the bundles off. They threw the bundles to the ground and opened them, taking out strange objects. Twisted Foot soon saw that they were making camp and he was surprised, for there was no water for the horses and not many miles away was the stream beside which he and Old Man Crazy had camped.

Two of the men got back on two of the horses, one of the brown ones and a gray, and this action attracted Twisted Foot's attention. He watched as they rode from the group into the grass, and he knew it was true that they could guide the horses where they wished. The two horses walked easily together and the men sat upright on their backs. Twisted Foot watched closely, wondering how it was done. Whatever the secret was, it escaped him, and presently he got to his feet and followed after the two men. He took care however not to get too close, for he did not wish to be seen.

The men rode over a nearby rise and were in the swale beyond when Twisted Foot reached the top. They went on a distance and then got off the horses. They left the horses standing and went on, carrying long black sticks and Twisted Foot knew from their cautious movements that they were stalking something. After a time, they halted. They placed the forked sticks upright in the ground and rested the longer black sticks in the forks. They bent their heads to the long sticks and presently there were loud sounds, like claps of thunder, and black smoke rolled forward from the ends of the sticks. Twisted Foot jumped as the sounds struck his ear drums, and then he knew what it was—the "smoke-sticks" which Old Man Crazy had told about, the strange sticks that Old Man Crazy said had the power to bring death at long distances.

Twisted Foot saw the white flashes of the rumps of the antelope as they fled. The men came back to their horses, jumped on them, and then Twisted Foot saw something that filled him with amazement. The two horses, carrying the men, raced after the antelope, and they ran with a speed which Twisted Foot would have believed impossible. They ran as fast as the antelope themselves. And the men on their backs leaned forward and yelled and kicked them in the sides with their feet, and obviously this was to encourage them in the running. Twisted Foot saw that their strides were long and smooth and powerful. Then the antelope and the men on the horses went over the next rise and were out of sight.

Twisted Foot waited a few minutes, wondering. Presently he heard another thunder clap, and he knew the two men were seeking to kill the antelope. He wondered why they did not use a flag and let the antelope come to them. He wondered how it was that the smoke-sticks could carry death at such long distances, even farther than an arrow. The men with the white skins possessed many unexplainable things.

No longer able to follow the men on the horses, Twisted Foot turned and made his way back to the rise, from which, in the late afternoon light, he could see the camp. The men were busy, moving about, putting things here and there. The horses, without their bundles and the leather harnesses, were feeding in the grass a short distance away and two of the men, each carrying a smoke-stick, were with them. Twisted Foot noticed that the horses, busy with their grazing, paid no attention to the men.

A short time later the two men who had gone out on the brown and gray horses came back, and on the horse in front of each of them there was an antelope carcass. They dumped the carcasses to the ground, got down, and began to take the back seats and the leather head harnesses from their horses. Twisted Foot noticed that the necks and shoulders of the horses were wet, and they were panting from the running. Their nostrils flared wide and one lowered its head and blew loudly to expel the dust. They rubbed their noses against the men in their impatience to be rid of the head harnesses, and when they were free, they sought a piece of dusty ground and lay down. They rolled on their backs and kicked their feet in the air, first on one side and then on the other. Twisted Foot decided, from having watched dogs go through similar motions, that they did this to dry their backs, which were wet where the seats had been. They got up presently and trotted eagerly toward those that were feeding, making soft impatient little sounds that came from deep in their throats.

The men gathered buffalo droppings that were well-dried and started fires. As it became darker, Twisted Foot crept closer. He was fascinated by these strange men, and the things they did and the strange articles they possessed. He noticed immediately that hair grew on the men's faces, even to the extent of covering their cheeks and mouths. And the skin above this hair, around their eyes, did not look very white. Nor did their hands. Their hands looked almost as dark as his own. He wondered how it was that they were known as the men with the white skins. Still, from Old Man Crazy's descriptions, he knew he could not be mistaken. Their skins, while not white, were different, and one even wore a hard bright shell about his upper body. This shell had two holes in it for the man's arms, and one for his neck, and Twisted Foot knew that an arrow would make a sound against it but would not go through, for that was what Old Man Crazy had told him. Old Man Crazy had said that sometimes the horses wore shells too, but these horses did not.

Two of the men skinned an antelope in the light of a fire. Twisted Foot watched them. Their movements were not very deft, but their knives were something he had never seen before. The blades were long, bright and mar- velously sharp, parting the red flesh with what seemed to be only the slightest pressure. And the meat was put in smoke-blackened vessels to cook over the fires instead of being suspended by strings or limbs. Twisted Foot won- dered why the vessels did not burn.

Now he could see their clothes clearly. They wore leg- gings and shirts made of a strange material. They wore

[142]

caps made of fur. Their hair was not long like his, but grew thick and bushy down their necks and about their ears, and the hair of some of them was yellow, as Old Man Crazy had said. Their moccasins were heavier and stiffer, and came up higher on their legs than any he had ever seen before.

But Twisted Foot was particularly interested in the leather harnesses which they put on the horses' heads, for he knew that these in some way had a function in the marvelous control. He could see one of the harnesses, where it lay on a pile of strange things, but it was too far from the fire to show clearly. A black smoke-stick lay against this pile too, and Twisted Foot noticed that it was slightly bent near the center, and wider at one end than at the other. He wondered how it made the loud noise, and wondered even more by what strange magic it could kill an antelope at a distance greater than an arrow's flight. In truth, these men with the white skins were strange and wondrous people.

As the men ate, they talked. Their voices sounded odd to Twisted Foot's ears and were often loud, as if in argument. They pointed and gestured with their arms, and occasionally one would leap abruptly to his feet and speak louder than the others. Twisted Foot could not make much of it, but they seemed displeased with one another.

They cooked a long time, and ate great quantities of the meat. After eating, they arranged their beds on the grass and lay down. The one who wore the bright shell

[143]

and another sat by a fire, talking in low tones after the others were asleep. The one with the bright shell had a thin, heavily-haired face with a high-bridged nose and deep set eyes, and he was tall and lean and obviously the leader of the party. Finally, these too went to their beds.

Twisted Foot still wished he could see one of the leather harnesses, but the light was so dim now that he could not make out the one on the pile. He considered the idea carefully. The men were asleep and he would not awaken them, nor would he do any harm.

Flat against the grass, Twisted Foot slid noiselessly forward. He went past the now faint coals of the fire and on to the pile. His hands found the harness and explored it. This was the loop that went over the horse's head and behind his ears. What was that, so hard and smooth? It was the thing that went in the horse's mouth, for he could feel the dried moisture on it. This thing puzzled him, for he could not understand its use. Then he felt the long strings that the men held in their hands. He had seen them pull on these. He put his hand on the black smoke-stick and found it hard and cold. How could it make the loud thunderclap? His hands touched a knife and he felt for the edge, finding it as thin and sharp as it had appeared when the men were butchering the antelope. He wondered how they could have made it, for no rock he knew was as thin and hard.

His curiosity presently satisfied, Twisted Foot wriggled on and out of the camp, his slim brown body barely making a rustle in the grass. He left the camp in the direction of the grazing horses, for he wished to look at them closer. Soon he could see their dark shapes. The white ones and the gray ones were clearer in the night. Twisted Foot got to his feet. The horses had shown no fear of the men with the white skins and he did not expect them to be afraid of him. But suddenly, as he approached closer, one gave a loud and startled snort.

Twisted Foot halted. Immediately a voice called out in the language of the men with the white skins. The voice called again, querulous and suspicious. Another voice answered. A horse snorted and there was nervous movement in the dark. Twisted Foot dropped to the grass and wriggled away, and he did not stop until he was well away from the horses.

Meanwhile the shouting had awakened the sleeping men and there was noise and confusion among them. They ran about in the darkness, calling to each other, and presently there came the thunderclaps of the smokesticks. Twisted Foot slipped silently away into the night.

CHAPTER THIRTEEN

TWISTED FOOT was filled with such astounding and exciting news that he had to tell someone. He set off through the dark in the direction of the stream. He walked steadily for some time before he came to the trees, dark in the night. He slipped among them, found the water's edge and drank. The camp he and Old Man Crazy had made was to his left, and he went in this direction, moving with habitual caution. After a time, he reached the camp. "Old Man? Old Man Crazy?" he called softly. "It is Twisted Foot, father."

There was no reply. Twisted Foot sniffed the air and found no odor of wood smoke or meat. He knew at once that Old Man Crazy was not there. He became concerned. It had been days since they had parted, but Old Man Crazy had said that he would wait. Twisted Foot scouted swiftly about the area, looking for a bed in the dark. He knew Old Man Crazy was sometimes a heavy sleeper. He found nothing.

Knowing there was nothing more he could do until day came, Twisted Foot selected a protected place in thick brush and went to sleep. He had traveled many miles since he had last rested and he slept soundly. But at daybreak he was awake. He hunted swiftly among the trees until he found a rabbit. He killed it and made a fire. It was not all he could have eaten, but it would do until he found Old Man Crazy.

A search of the brush revealed that Old Man Crazy had spent much time at the place after they had parted. As Twisted Foot had known he would, the old man had turned to snares for food, and there were the bones of rabbits and mice and other small animals, and also feathers of ground-running birds. The ashes at the fire spot were deep. Then, on the ground near the ashes, Twisted Foot noticed three small sticks, arranged in the shape of an arrow and pointing up the stream. He hurried in that direction and had not gone far when Old Man Crazy's creaky voice said, "Where is the rope, little brother?"

Old Man Crazy was lying on an antelope skin, on the sunny side of a young thicket. His brown old body looked thinner than ever to Twisted Foot and the lines in his face seemed deeper. "Have you no meat?" Twisted Foot asked with some concern. He knew then why Old Man Crazy had moved, because the small creatures had become scarce about the other camp.

"There will be something in my snares," Old Man Crazy said. He pushed himself slowly up to a sitting position. "Why did you not bring the rope, little brother?" he went on, disappointment in his voice. "I wished to make a big snare again so the Comanches would have a horse."

Twisted Foot could not contain his great news any longer. "The men with the white skins are come, father," he said.

Old Man Crazy's single eye squinted dully. "The men with the white skins are far away."

"No they are not," Twisted Foot said emphatically. "They are come."

"It cannot be," Old Man Crazy said wearily.

"It is," Twisted Foot insisted. "I saw them, on the prairie. They have horses with them, many horses."

"It was buffalo," Old Man Crazy said. "I have seen the men with the white skins, but it was long ago and far away."

"It was not buffalo, father," Twisted Foot said insistently. "The men with the white skins are come."

"How close did you see them?" Old Man Crazy asked, striving to be patient.

"Very close. Within an arrow's flight," Twisted Foot said.

"And their skins were white?" Old Man Crazy said.

"Yes, father," Twisted Foot said, knowing it to be true.

"Did you see their skins?"

"No," Twisted Foot admitted. "Their bodies were covered. But I am certain it was they, father. I remembered what you said about them. One wore a shining shell, as you have told."

"What color were their faces?" Old Man Crazy asked. "Surely their faces were not covered also."

"They were—with hair," Twisted Foot answered.

"Hair?" Old Man Crazy cried, sitting bolt upright. "Did you see hair on their faces?"

"Yes," Twisted Foot said. "It was below their eyes, about their mouths. Why did you not tell me of that before, father?"

"And they had horses?" Old Man Crazy said, still finding it difficult to believe.

"Yes," Twisted Foot told him. "They rode on the horses' backs. There were harnesses on the horses' heads. Two of them were white . . ."

"Where is this?" Old Man Crazy interrupted impatiently. "I would see it."

"On the prairie."

"What is the distance?" Old Man Crazy asked. "I have told Kills Something and our people of this, and they would not believe me. Sometimes I did not believe myself, it was so strange. Now I will see it once more. I will learn how it is that the men with white skins have horses and the horses obey their wishes. Then our people can no longer doubt me. Where is this, little brother?" He pushed himself to his thin bent legs.

"I was there last darkness," Twisted Foot told him.

"Come. We will go," Old Man Crazy said eagerly. He threw the antelope skin to his shoulder.

"You have not yet eaten," Twisted Foot reminded him. "Make a fire. I will get some meat."

"No," Old Man Crazy said. "That can wait. We will eat later. Let us go at once. Lead the way." He was insistent.

"We will go, father," Twisted Foot said. "But first we must drink deeply. Do not forget the prairie is dry." He led the way to the stream and lay down at the edge.

Old Man Crazy got down too and drank. He finished quickly and said, "Lead the way, little brother. I would hurry."

"You will soon be thirsty," Twisted Foot warned.

"Lead the way," Old Man Crazy cried angrily. "I know when I am full. The men with the white skins will not stay long in one place."

Twisted Foot left the trees and took a course directly across the grass. Old Man Crazy followed closely at his heels. "Tell me when you see them, little brother," Old Man Crazy said presently.

"It will be a long while yet," Twisted Foot told him.

They pushed on steadily. After several miles Twisted Foot would have halted to permit Old Man Crazy to rest, but Old Man Crazy, with a surprising show of strength, was impatiently at his heels.

Another hour passed. Twisted Foot halted and said, "There are antelope, father. We could eat the liver."

"There will be time to eat later," Old Man Crazy said. "Keep going."

[150]

The sun reached a place high in the sky and heat waves began dancing over the sea of brown grass. Old Man Crazy spread his antelope skin across his scrawny shoulders. Twisted Foot came to a dry wash, where a cut bank provided a strip of shade. He squatted in this.

"Why are you halting?" Old Man Crazy demanded crossly.

"There is something I would tell you, father," Twisted Foot said earnestly. "Sit here beside me."

Old Man Crazy sat down, grumbling.

"I will recover the rope, father," Twisted Foot told him.

"How?" Old Man Crazy asked. "Where is it?"

"On the horse," Twisted Foot said.

"On the horse?" Old Man Crazy repeated in surprise. "How do you know?"

"I saw it. It is still about the horse's neck. It will not fall off."

"Then how will you recover it?"

"I will catch the horse," Twisted Foot said. "I will catch the horse and take the rope from its neck."

"It is a foolish dream," Old Man Crazy said impatiently. "You cannot run."

"The horse will let me catch it," Twisted Foot said. "I know that, father. Already I have had my hands on its head. It likes to have its ears scratched. I have named it Likes-His-Ears-Scratched."

Old Man Crazy was too astounded to speak for several

seconds. "How did you do it, little brother?" he asked
presently.

Twisted Foot realized that he did not know, not exactly.
"It just happened," he said. "I followed him to get the
rope, and he became not afraid any longer. And I was
not afraid. It is a strange thing, but it is true, father."

"Are you certain?" Old Man Crazy asked. "You have
had your hands on its head, and it did not flee?"

"Yes, father."

Old Man Crazy was thoughtful. "What did you say
you named it?" he asked presently.

"Likes-His-Ears-Scratched," Twisted Foot said. "It is
his name."

"He will do your bidding?" Old Man Crazy demanded,
doubt returning to his voice.

"Yes, father," Twisted Foot said. "I will teach him the
Comanche words. Already he listens to my voice. When
he knows the words he will obey. You will see it. I will
take the rope from his neck."

"The rope is not important any more," Old Man Crazy
said. "It was to catch a horse that I wished it."

"It has caught a horse," Twisted Foot said. "It is on the
horse's neck now."

"Where is the horse?" Old Man Crazy asked.

"At a water hole. I left it there," Twisted Foot said.

"How do you know it will be there when you return?"
Old Man Crazy asked pointedly.

"I do not know," Twisted Foot said. "But he will be

there. If he is not, I will follow him. I will follow him until I find him. He knows I will come back."

"He cannot know that," Old Man Crazy said. "You could not tell him."

"No, but he knows it," Twisted Foot replied confidently.

Old Man Crazy was silent a few seconds, then said, "We will go first to see the men with white skins. They understand how to control horses, and there is much we must learn, little brother."

"Yes, father," Twisted Foot said. "I saw the men on the backs of the horses. It was difficult to believe. The horses followed the antelope at great speed."

"Did I not tell Kills Something so?" Old Man Crazy said stoutly.

"The men brought antelope back on the horses," Twisted Foot said.

Old Man Crazy nodded and said, "The men with white skins have taught them many things. It is of great importance."

"Will the men with the white skins tell us?" Twisted Foot asked. "How can they, since the tongue they speak is different?"

Old Man Crazy hesitated. "I do not know. Many winters have passed since I saw these men, and I do not know. But it is of great importance. It is in my mind not to ask at first, but to watch. Much may be learned from watching, little brother."

"Yes," Twisted Foot agreed.

They left the dry wash and went on across the rolling plain. Twisted Foot remembered the direction the men with the white skins had been following, and he laid a course to intercept them on their morning march.

"I see dust, father," he said after a while.

"Where? Where is it?" Old Man Crazy cried eagerly.

"There," Twisted Foot said, pointing.

Old Man Crazy strained his one eye into the distance for a second, then shook his head angrily and said, "Lead to it, little brother."

The procession was not as far along as Twisted Foot had believed it would be and he turned to meet it. After a time, he could see the dark objects which he knew to be men and horses. He did not tell Old Man Crazy, for he realized that Old Man Crazy could not see them.

They came presently to another dry wash, a deep, narrow, twisting channel cut in the surface of the prairie by past cloudbursts. Its shoulder-high walls were steep and its bottom was of firm sand.

"Perhaps it is best we wait at this place, father," Twisted Foot told Old Man Crazy. "They will come this way and will pass near by."

"Where are they now?" Old Man Crazy said. "I would see them."

"There. They are there," Twisted Foot said, pointing.

"I cannot see them," Old Man Crazy said exasperatedly.

[154]

"It is some distance yet," Twisted Foot told him. "But they will pass near by."

Old Man Crazy grumbled under his breath and sat down on the sand. The sun was warm but he pulled his antelope skin about his narrow shoulders. "Tell me when they come, little brother," he said.

Twisted Foot watched the approaching caravan. A man on one of the brown horses was in the front. He was the one who wore the bright shell and he kept turning his head from side to side. Twisted Foot wondered what he might be looking for. The other men and other horses were behind these two, and they moved with a weary indifference.

"Is it yet, little brother?" Old Man Crazy asked from his place in the wash.

"No, father," Twisted Foot answered. He was lying upon the lip of the bank, where he could watch over the grass. "They move like pack dogs at the end of a long day."

The men with the white skins came on and presently, while still some distance from Twisted Foot, the one in front halted and the others came forward and gathered about him.

"They have stopped now," Twisted Foot told Old Man Crazy.

"For what reason?" Old Man Crazy asked, struggling to his feet.

"I do not know," Twisted Foot said. "They talk and wave their arms. They act as if they are not sure of where they are. I believe that is the reason. There was no water where they halted for the past night."

"We will tell them of the stream," Old Man Crazy said. "They can go to it."

"Yes," Twisted Foot said.

"They will thank us for it," Old Man Crazy said, nodding his head to himself.

"They come on now," Twisted Foot said.

Old Man Crazy climbed up to a place beside him. "Where? Where are they?"

"There," Twisted Foot said, pointing.

Old Man Crazy looked, then said, "I cannot see them."

"They will come nearer," Twisted Foot told him. "They will pass very close."

"The sun is hot," Old Man Crazy said. "The heat waves dance before my eyes."

"You have only one, father," Twisted Foot said.

"No, I have two," Old Man Crazy said. "But I cannot see. Do the men still come?"

"Yes," Twisted Foot said. "They will soon be before us."

The men with the white skins came on, a compact little group, led by the tall man on the brown horse. The horses' feet stirred the dry ground and the dust floated up and hung in the still air. Some of the men walked and carried the long smoke-sticks in their hands.

"They are there, father," Twisted Foot told Old Man Crazy. "They are very near now."

"Where?" Old Man Crazy said eagerly, lifting his head to look.

"There," Twisted Foot said. It amazed him that Old Man Crazy, even with his poor vision, could not see the men, for he remembered when Old Man Crazy had seen antelope at longer distances. "There, father."

"I cannot see them," Old Man Crazy said excitedly. "I must get nearer." He lurched up to his feet and started across the grass.

"Wait," Twisted Foot called, concerned and uncertain. Old Man Crazy did not pause, but moved on toward the men with the white skins. Twisted Foot got to his feet and followed Old Man Crazy, hurrying to catch up.

"I must see them, so that once more I can tell Kills Something and our people," Old Man Crazy said determinedly. "Where are they now, little brother?"

"There," Twisted Foot said, pointing. He took Old Man Crazy by the arm to guide him.

The men with the white skins halted and quickly formed a little group. Twisted Foot could see that they were watching him and Old Man Crazy, and he became worried. "Wait," he said to Old Man Crazy.

But Old Man Crazy would not wait. Twisted Foot saw the dark blowing of smoke, and he heard a flat slap against Old Man Crazy's bony chest. He heard the thunderclap. Old Man Crazy suddenly lost his strength and sagged to

[157]

the ground, dragging Twisted Foot down with him. Twisted Foot was shocked and confused.

"The smoke-stick," Old Man Crazy mumbled weakly. "Did I not tell Kills Something of it?"

Twisted Foot saw the small hole in Old Man Crazy's chest, a hole from which blood bubbled brightly. He heard a passing, as of a hurrying bee, in the air above his head, and close behind came another thunder clap.

Old Man Crazy wrenched up on a skinny elbow, and his eye was calm and clear. "Run, little brother, run," he said firmly.

"But, father . . ." Twisted Foot began, perplexed and grieving.

"Run!" Old Man Crazy ordered angrily. "*You* must escape." It took the last of his strength and he fell back to the grass.

Twisted Foot threw himself to the grass. He heard still another thunder clap, and he heard shouts and yells from the men with the white skins. He wriggled through the grass and in a few seconds was over the lip and into the wash. Then, ducked low, he ran along the firm sandy bottom.

CHAPTER FOURTEEN

TWISTED FOOT heard a pounding of hoofs. He knew it was one of the men with white skins riding along the wash, looking for him. He threw himself against the base of a cut bank and lay there, tightly, while the pounding passed, then he leaped up, over the rim and into the grass. The grass was short, but Twisted Foot's body was slim and he knew he could not remain in the wash, for that was where the men would look. He slithered through the grass for some distance, then caught a glimpse of the rider coming back, this time on the far side of the wash. Twisted Foot became limp and motionless, a trick the Indians had learned from baby antelope, and neither the horse nor man saw him.

The men searched along the wash for some time, calling and shouting to each other, then they gathered back where Old Man Crazy had fallen. A big lump came into Twisted Foot's throat, for he knew Old Man Crazy was dead. He could not understand why the men with the white skins had done it. Old Man Crazy had meant them no harm. And they had tried to kill him, Twisted Foot, too. He pondered on it a long time and could reach no answer save that the men with the white skins were bad people. Even the Utes did not make war unless there was a reason.

Presently, the men went back to their horses and got on their backs and went on, moving slowly as before. Twisted Foot waited until they were out of sight, over a rise; he waited until he was certain they were not coming back, then he went to Old Man Crazy. The old Indian's body seemed thinner and more shriveled than ever as it lay there in the grass, causing Twisted Foot to wonder how it had ever held such a bold and driving spirit.

The men with the white skins had taken the antelope skin, and the old worn stone knife. They had even taken the wrinkled old moccasins. Twisted Foot thought about this for several seconds, then took off his own moccasins and put them on Old Man Crazy's feet. The round one did not fit well, but at least Old Man Crazy would not be barefooted when he arrived among the spirit people.

There were no stones or trees, nothing that could be used to dig, so Twisted Foot carried Old Man Crazy to the wash and laid him straight at the foot of a steep bank. He put his antelope flag over Old Man Crazy's lined face and folded Old Man Crazy's arms across his chest. Then he climbed to the top of the bank and caved down dirt until the small brown body was completely covered. The old Comanche rested at last.

Twisted Foot turned across the prairie, picking his way with bare feet over the grass. He felt small and much alone, and there was a great sadness in his heart. He walked indifferently, discouraged and weary. But presently he straightened and moved with more spirit. Likes-His-Ears-Scratched would be waiting for him at the water hole.

You must escape, Old Man Crazy had said, and now Twisted Foot knew why the old Indian had been so insistent. He, Twisted Foot, was the one now who must tell the Comanches, tell them about the men with the white skins and their unfriendliness, about the smoke-sticks and the marvel of the horses. He would do better than merely tell them about the horses; he would take one to show them. Perhaps Old Man Crazy had that in his mind too.

Twisted Foot saw a rabbit hiding under a clump of grass. He put an arrow in his bow and killed it. The meat would be welcome for his supper that night and the skin could be used for an antelope flag.

It was long after dark when he arrived at the water hole. A drumming of small hooves told him that he had surprised drinking antelope. He listened intently for the pounding of heavier round hoofs, but heard none. He went among the shadows calling softly, "Likes-Your-Ears-Scratched . . . Likes-Your-Ears-Scratched . . ." He circled the water hole completely but did not find the stallion, and this caused him some concern. If the horse were gone too, life would be almost unbearably pointless.

He cooked and ate the rabbit, then got the bobcat skin from its hiding place and spread it for a bed. At daylight he was up. He looked about under the trees, then went barefooted to the open. The brown stallion was not in sight, in any direction that he looked. He walked around the trees, with no better results. Now he became keenly worried. He had not believed the stallion would leave, and wondered if something evil could have happened to him.

Leaving the trees, Twisted Foot made a circle over the grass. The grass close in had been grazed down and Twisted Foot widened his circle to the taller grass. Here, presently, he struck outgoing sign, and his fingers exploring in the grass roots told him it had been made by hard round hoofs. He followed the trail. It led over a small rise and into the next swale. Here the horse had grazed for a time before moving on. The trail led into sparse grass, over flinty ground, and Twisted Foot had difficulty in following it. He went slowly, searching it out. Finally, it became so tedious that he left it and went on to the highest crest in the vicinity. Here he looked for an hour, but could see nothing of the brown stallion. He looked until his eyes ached, and his heart ached too. But the stallion was not in sight. He did see something, however, that quickened his pulse, a low stain of dust against the blue of the sky far to the west. It told him that the men with the white skins had altered their course. He didn't like this, for it would bring them too close to the water hole, and he did not want to see them again. He knew now that they were his enemies, worse than the Utes. But in his anxiety to find the horse, he soon dismissed the dust cloud from his mind.

He saw some antelope and this reminded him that he needed both meat and skin. He put the rabbit pelt up on a pole and lay beneath it. An hour later he killed a fat buck. He ate the liver immediately, then carried the rest of the animal back to the swale where he had left the trail. Now he was determined to puzzle it out, to follow it, regardless of the time and effort required, for he knew that it would lead him to Likes-His-Ears-Scratched. That was the single encouraging certainty left for him to cling to. Old Man Crazy would not speak to him again, but the brown stallion was at the end of that faint line of sign.

The trail did not become any easier to read and, despite his eagerness, Twisted Foot made slow progress. Finally, darkness made it impossible for him to continue. He went back unhappily and took up the antelope. There was nothing left but to go back to the water hole and return again in the morning. Tomorrow he would find Likes-His-Ears-Scratched; he had to, for he could not break faith with Old Man Crazy.

Reaching the lake, Twisted Foot made a good fire. While it burned to cooking coals, he skinned the antelope and cut two pieces of the hide for moccasins. He hung a big piece of meat over the fire and let it roast as he continued working on the moccasins. One he shaped round, for his deformed foot. He made them big and roomy, knowing that the green hide would shrink as it dried. They were poor makeshifts when compared to those his mother made, but they would protect his feet until he could properly cure a hide. Now, another matter was of much greater importance.

Twisted Foot was up at the first light of morning. He ate a quick breakfast, drank all the water he could hold, and started back to the swale in which he had been forced to quit the trail. Going toward the trees, he saw a movement. He halted, quickly alert, and then his heart sang, for coming in from the grass was Likes-His-Ears-Scratched.

"Ooooohhoooo," Twisted Foot crooned happily. "You did come back. You did come back. Where have you been? I have looked everywhere. You did come back."

The horse halted, raised his head and then, to Twisted Foot's keen delight, gave a soft nicker of pleasure. Twisted Foot went toward him. Likes-His-Ears-Scratched arched his neck, showing signs of nervousness, either feigned or real. Twisted Foot halted and put out his hand. "Do not run," he said. "It is Twisted Foot. I have come back to you. I will not hurt Likes-His-Ears-Scratched."

The stallion stretched his neck forward cautiously and Twisted Foot held his hand to be smelled. The stallion's nostrils flared as he drew the air in deeply and then the nervousness went out of him. He took a step forward and lowered his head. Twisted Foot began to scratch gently at the base of the horse's trim ears.

[165]

"I knew you would remember," Twisted Foot told him. He was very proud and he wished Old Man Crazy could see him now. Old Man Crazy would know that he had won, that a Comanche had a horse at last. Of course there was still much to be taught and much to learn, but he could do it. He had watched the hated men with the white skins and had seen how they rode. He could do it too, though he wished he had one of those leather harnesses they had put on their horses' heads. He decided that he would make one, from antelope hide. He was certain he could do it, though he didn't have one of those little hard sticks that went in the horses' mouths. He would have to think about that.

Just now, however, he was busy re-establishing himself with Likes-His-Ears-Scratched. He scratched and rubbed and ran his fingers through the stallion's thick mane. The rope was still about the stallion's neck, its end becoming frayed from being stepped on. Twisted Foot remembered that he had seen the horses with bundles on their backs following the men with white skins by a rope. On impulse, he took the rope in his hand. Likes-His-Ears-Scratched seemed not to notice, and when Twisted Foot gave a tentative pull on the rope, the horse responded by stepping forward. Twisted Foot leaped back, to keep from being trod on, and Likes-His-Ears-Scratched kept coming. Twisted Foot turned and Likes-His-Ears-Scratched followed, and kept following. Twisted Foot went some distance, realizing joyously that he had learned one secret.

Now he could get Likes-His-Ears-Scratched to follow him. But how to stop him? Twisted Foot was not certain of that. It took courage for him to halt in front of the horse, but he did. "Stop," he said in Comanche. "Stop." And he pushed back on the rope, though knowing this would do no good. But, wonder of wonders, Likes-His-Ears-Scratched stopped.

Twisted Foot scratched the stallion's ears a minute longer, then dropped the rope. He could not stand much more just then, for there was great trembling and happiness in him. He needed time to think, to consider the fine progress, and make certain he was doing nothing wrong.

Released, the stallion sought the shade of a tree. Twisted Foot stood near the water, watching. Now the horse would follow him but how, on its back, could he make it go forward? And how could he be certain of staying on its back? These were things that would need much thinking about. He wished Old Man Crazy were here to help him, for Old Man Crazy had been a great one to think.

Then something else came to Twisted Foot's mind. He turned and went through the trees. He climbed to the crest of a rise. There it was, the dust cloud he had seen the previous afternoon, only now it was much nearer. It was so near that already he could see the dark objects at its base. He frowned, deeply worried. Could it be buffalo, or was it the men with the white skins?

Twisted Foot kept watching. The dark objects disappeared, and he knew they had entered a swale for he could still see the dust cloud. The cloud seemed to be standing still, but it did not dwindle and when, after some time, the dark objects appeared again, they were much closer. Twisted Foot saw that one was white, and another one. His heart sank miserably. From his recent experience with the men with white skins, he was certain that if they found him, they would shoot him, as they had Old Man Crazy, and worse still, they would take Likes-His-Ears-Scratched. He himself could hide and slip away through the grass, but Likes-His-Ears-Scratched could not slip through the grass. In the open, Likes-His-Ears-Scratched could be seen from a long distance.

But maybe, Twisted Foot thought, hope rising, the men with the white skins would not come to the water hole. They were moving in a direction which would take them past it. So he remained still and watched, and hoped they would go by. The men and horses moved on, strung out behind their leader. It looked as if they were surely going to pass the water hole, when suddenly one of the horses halted and raised its head. It was one with a bundle, one of the gray ones. It looked for a few seconds, then started toward the water hole, trotting in its eagerness. Then men and other horses turned immediately to follow it.

Twisted Foot knew longer waiting was hopeless. He turned and ran as fast as his deformed foot would let him go to the trees. He went inside, out of sight. What now? He glanced about desperately. He could hide and escape.

But the men with the white skins would get Likes-His-Ears-Scratched, and Old Man Crazy's dream would go for nothing. He ran toward the horse. Likes-His-Ears-Scratched threw up his head and ears, warning Twisted Foot. Twisted Foot slowed to a walk and forced himself to be calm. "I will not hurt you," he said. "I have come to take you away, so the men with the white skins will not get you. They killed Old Man Crazy, and they will kill me if they can catch me. If you stay here, they will take you and the rope."

The stallion stood, permitting him to come up. He paused to scratch the horse's ears before reaching for the rope. "Good," he said. "Now we will go."

But before he could turn, an eager plaintive nicker sounded out on the plain. Likes-His-Ears-Scratched jerked up his head and sent forth a trumpeting reply, a cry of joyous welcome, filled with pent-up loneliness for his own kind. Twisted Foot was shocked and dismayed, and knew immediately that all hopes he might have had for slipping away undiscovered were ruined. To make it still worse, Likes-His-Ears-Scratched started eagerly to meet the other horse. Twisted Foot knew he couldn't permit this. He hung doggedly to the rope and the stallion's head came around.

"Come," Twisted Foot said firmly. "Come, Likes-Your-Ears-Scratched. We must go."

The horse resisted, his head still up and his ears pointed in the direction from which the nicker had come.

[169]

Twisted Foot was desperate. He pulled hard on the rope. "Come!" he cried. "Come, Likes-Your-Ears-Scratched. The men with the white skins will get you!"

The stallion followed, but reluctantly, turning his head to look back. Twisted Foot started around the little lake, to leave the trees from the far side where he would have the best chance of being unobserved. He hurried as fast as he could, pulling hard at the rope, but Likes-His-Ears-Scratched would not hurry.

A horse burst from the trees behind them and despite Twisted Foot's efforts, the stallion swung to a halt and neighed an eager welcome. The horse did not answer but hurried to the water and pushed its nose in deep to drink. It was the gray, with a big bundle on its back.

"Come," Twisted Foot cried desperately, pulling at the rope. "We must go. We must hurry."

The stallion came around and followed him, but turned his head again to neigh. The drinking horse raised its head, looked, and made a soft noise in its throat. It put its head down again. "Come," Twisted Foot said, and put all of his strength against the rope. The stallion followed him and they entered the trees.

At the far edge, Twisted Foot paused briefly to glance out. The plain was empty. He led Likes-His-Ears-Scratched forward and headed straight, anxious to get away from the water hole as quickly as possible. Before he had gone more than a short distance, he heard a pounding of hoofs behind and the sound sent terror to his heart.

"Come on," he cried, going as fast as the stallion would follow, which was much too slow. The horse kept trying to look back. Out of the corner of his eye, Twisted Foot saw a horse break from the trees and come toward them, running fast.

He whirled, feeling trapped but determined somehow not to lose his horse. Then he saw that the horse following them so anxiously did not have a man on its back but a bundle. It was the gray.

Relieved, Twisted Foot said, "Come, come," and led as rapidly as Likes-His-Ears-Scratched would follow. The gray horse came fast and caught up quickly. It nickered happily and followed beside the stallion. Twisted Foot was annoyed by its presence but soon discovered that Likes-His-Ears-Scratched followed much more willingly. They hurried across the grass. The stallion presently increased his gait to a trot, for which Twisted Foot was greatly thankful. They made better progress, but the gray horse trotted too and kept close behind. Twisted Foot wished it would go back, for he knew the men with the white skins would be more certain to follow. Also, two horses would be more readily seen than one. But he knew no way to keep it from coming.

They went on and on, and the distance back to the trees increased until presently Twisted Foot began to be hopeful that the men with the white skins had not discovered them, and that somehow they did not know that the horse with the bundle was following them. He was

[171]

hopeful, too, because it was late in the afternoon and when darkness came, it would hide them. He hurried on, and the stallion trotted behind him and the horse with the bundle trotted beside the stallion.

But when he glanced back a short time later, he knew his hopes were in vain. Two more horses had emerged from the trees and were coming fast. There was a third horse behind them. And these carried men on their backs, the men with the white skins.

"Come on! Hurry!" he cried at the stallion, and went as fast as he could. But the stallion merely trotted with his head in the air and held Twisted Foot back.

Twisted Foot glanced again and desperately at the men behind. They were coming across the grass swiftly. It would be only a matter of minutes until they caught him, and he saw that they carried smoke-sticks in their hands. He felt weak with discouragement. There was no place to hide, no chance to escape. He could drop to the grass and lie still. But Likes-His-Ears-Scratched was certain to be caught and taken. Twisted Foot felt that he might as well be killed himself. Then suddenly a thought flashed into his mind, a daring thought. Could he? Did he have the courage? His knees turned weak, for he knew he wasn't ready for it yet. Still he had to do it. It was the only possible way. He gulped down his fear. It had to be now, or it never would be. There was no time left to think. Still holding the rope, he grabbed both hands full of the long neck hair and scrambled up on the stallion's back.

He gripped frantically with his legs and feet and cried in shrill Comanche, "Go! Go!"

Likes-His-Ears-Scratched may not have understood the words but he could not mistake the tone, or the urgency of those digging heels. And the thunderclap of a smoke-stick behind may have hastened him too. At any rate, a mighty strength went into action under Twisted Foot and the grass of the prairie began to flow backward. There was another thunderclap, still farther behind.

The long neck hair stung Twisted Foot's face. He was scared but determined. His hands were locked in the horse's mane and his feet and legs were clenched as tightly as he could hold them. He hung on and dared not look at the dizzying ground. There was a pounding of hoofs be-hind, but this was lost in the pounding of his own blood in his temples. He was conscious of only one thing—that he must not fall. He clung tightly and the stallion's feet began to beat a steady rhythm . . . *faster than any man can run* . . .

Later, much later, and in the growing darkness, when Twisted Foot's hands and arms and legs were aching, the stallion slowed his pace, first to a rough, jolting trot and presently to a walk. Twisted Foot was exhausted with holding on. "Stop," he cried. "Stop, Likes-Your-Ears-Scratched."

The stallion halted and Twisted Foot tumbled to the ground, thoroughly shaken by the experience. Excess blood was in his feet and he stumbled and fell, but he held to the rope and was up quickly. He did not know what had become of the men with the white skins, and could only assume that they had been left behind. He hoped so—far behind. Yet he could not be sure, for the gray mare was still with them. She had galloped steadily after the stallion all the while and now came to a blowing, panting stop, her high pack looming in the darkness.

Twisted Foot listened for more hoof beats and peered into the gathering night. He could neither hear nor see anything of the men with white skins, and for this he was thankful beyond words. Nevertheless, he was taking nothing for granted. He glanced up at the stars for direction, then said to the stallion, "Come," and turned to the west. They moved off through the gloom, limping youth and hot sweaty horse. The gray mare gazed after them a few seconds, then followed, determined not to be left alone. Once she paused and glanced back, as if wondering what had become of the others.

CHAPTER FIFTEEN

SOMETIME DEEP in the night, Twisted Foot came to a stream, the same one by which he and Old Man Crazy had had their camp. He halted in the gloom of the trees. Now he felt some security from pursuit by the men with the white skins, and also he was weary. It had been an exciting day, one which still left him a bit breathless when he thought about it. And he was keenly proud of Likes-His-Ears-Scratched, for the brown horse had measured up to the need in a manner more gallant than Twisted Foot would have dared to dream. Likes-His-Ears-Scratched had saved them both.

The gray mare pushed on to the water to drink and the stallion tugged at the rope to join her. Twisted Foot went with him and stood regarding the mare, wondering why she had come. He wished she had not, for he felt that the men with the white skins would be less persistent in their pursuit. But here she was and there seemed little he could do about it. On the other hand, Likes-His-Ears-Scratched, long without the companionship of other horses, was obviously calmed and pleased by her presence.

The horses finished drinking and the mare turned and made her way through the heavy shadows to the thick grass, where immediately she began to graze. Twisted Foot realized that the animals needed food, and he led Likes-His-Ears-Scratched to the grass too. The stallion ate hungrily, clipping the grass with his strong teeth. Twisted Foot held the rope, too excited and too uncertain to turn it loose. He followed wherever Likes-His-Ears-Scratched wanted to go.

The mare had neither rope nor halter, but indicated no desire to leave. Twisted Foot looked at the bundle on her back and remembered seeing the men with the white skins untie the leather straps and take the bundles down. He felt that the mare would be pleased to have him take this bundle from her back, but he was reluctant to touch it, not knowing what strange magic it might contain.

Twisted Foot was so tired that presently he sat down and, fearing that he might go to sleep, he tied the end of the rope about his wrist. He did go to sleep, almost immediately. When he awoke, it seemed that he had slept only a minute but the horses had ceased to eat and stood drowsing on their feet. Though it was still dark, Twisted Foot realized that it would not be long until morning. And morning could bring many things, including the dreaded men with the white skins.

Twisted Foot got to his feet. "Come," he said to the stallion, and tugged at the rope. The horse awoke and turned after him, and the gray mare, still with her pack, followed behind.

At the water's edge Twisted Foot let the horses drink again and drank himself. He led them into the water and across it and presently left the trees at the far side. He struck straight across the prairie. The sky turned silver and the sun came up. Twisted Foot paused on a rise to scan the country behind and was pleased that he could see no men on horses.

After several hours he came to another stream, this one smaller and with less trees and brush about it. He looked behind carefully again, then led the stallion into the cover. The mare followed them, obviously welcoming the shade. Twisted Foot was still unwilling to turn Likes-His-Ears-Scratched loose, so he tied the rope firmly to a stout tree. He looked at the mare, wondering about her, for his natural caution told him that she too should be kept in the cover during the day. In the open she might bring the men with the white skins straight to his hiding place.

He had no other rope, however, and nothing just then that he could use to make one. He noticed the bundle, and the long strong strap that tied it to the horse. The strap could take the place of a rope, if he could get it. He approached the mare cautiously, saying, "I want to get a strap. I will not hurt you." She showed no nervousness whatever. Twisted Foot found the knot and untied it. The strap came loose, but there was another knot. He went around the horse and untied that one also. He tugged at the strap and, suddenly, the bundle and all came down. Twisted Foot leaped to one side, and the bundle hit the ground with a clashing, clanging sound such as he had never heard before. He regarded the bundle suspiciously for several seconds, fearing some more of the magic of the men with white skins. But nothing happened, save that the mare turned her head and rubbed him with her nose in obvious appreciation of being relieved of the burden, and this started a new feeling toward her in Twisted Foot's mind. She was a nice horse, though of course not so wonderful as Likes-His-Ears-Scratched, who was sleeping through all this. She had a high pack-saddle on her back. Twisted Foot knew this had been for the bundle to rest on, and he took it off.

After tying the mare with the long strap, Twisted Foot turned his attention to the bundle. It was wrapped in what looked to be a big hide, but really wasn't leather at all. Twisted Foot didn't know what it was, for he had never seen cloth before. He took an edge and pulled gently, somewhat apprehensively. The cloth came away and Twisted Foot's eyes opened wide. It was shiny hard shells, such as the tall man with white skin had worn and which Old Man Crazy had often described. Twisted Foot touched one with his finger and was surprised by its smoothness and hardness. He wondered how the men with the white skins had made it. This piece, he could tell from the shape, was for the upper body, and there were two long pieces that he could not place until he noticed that the ends were shaped like moccasins, only with long pointed toes. The remaining piece had to be for the head. Twisted Foot tried it on and discovered, though it was much too big for him, that there were holes he could see through. It was heavy and uncomfortable and he soon took it off. But he could see its advantage in battle, for a man wearing all the pieces could not be hurt by arrows or lances. This was more of the magic of the men with white skins.

Twisted Foot was too hungry to spend much time with the armor. He killed a rabbit, made a small fire and cooked it. After eating, he left the trees, went back to the first rise, and stayed there for some time, watching the country. He then returned to the trees and stretched out in the shade near the horses. In a few minutes he was asleep.

It was late in the afternoon when Twisted Foot awoke. He lay still a few seconds, listening. The horses were restless at their ties and he knew they were hungry. He got up and went to the edge of the trees. After a few seconds, he moved on to a rise and looked for any sign of the men with white skins. Presently he returned to the trees, turned the mare loose, untied Likes-His-Ears-Scratched and led him out to grass. The horses began to feed hungrily. Twisted Foot remained with them, holding the stallion's rope. He was not yet sure enough of Likes-His-Ears-Scratched to let him feed loose. As for the mare, he knew she would not leave and he would not have been much concerned if she had.

When the horses began to show signs of being full, Twisted Foot took them back to the trees, watered and tied them. He hunted along the stream for his own supper and presently surprised a beaver on the bank and killed it. He took it back near the horses, made a small fire and roasted it, pleased to have the rich juicy meat.

It was dark by the time he had finished and he sat by the fire, considering what he should do. This was a good place, cover and grass being plentiful for the horses. But he was worried about the men with the white skins, believing they would not hesitate to kill him and take the horses if they could find him. And he wasn't ready for another wild ride, like the one of the previous day.

He went to the mare to untie her and noticed the pile of bright armor. He stopped and frowned, wondering what he should do with it. He could see no value in it and left it where it lay, but he did tie the pad and the heavy cloth on the mare's back, thinking that he could find some use for them.

Twisted Foot traveled most of the night, leading the stallion. The mare followed readily with her reduced burden. Once Twisted Foot considered getting on the stallion's back, but he decided against it, remembering his fright and helplessness the other time. It would come later, when he had more time to think about it.

The stallion pulled back on the rope and halted. His

raised nostrils pulled in the night air. Twisted Foot listened but could hear nothing. The gray mare turned through the night, leading the way. Twisted Foot followed her, cautiously. Presently, he too could smell the water.

It was a spring, in a narrow little canyon at the base of a steep face of weathered brown stone. The horses drank while Twisted Foot looked about. There were not as many trees as he could have wished for, but the brush was dense and green. Too, day would soon be coming. He tied Likes-His-Ears-Scratched and took the pack saddle and bundle cover off the mare. She moved out of the brush and began to feed. Twisted Foot led Likes-His-Ears-Scratched after her. He let them eat until the sky lightened in the east, then took the stallion back and tied him. He got the strap and went after the mare, who remained at the grass. "I must tie you," he told her. "You cannot stay out here in the open where you might be seen." She stood quietly while he walked up to her, and followed willingly back to the trees.

Twisted Foot noticed with satisfaction that the little canyon was well hidden from surrounding view. It began at the small face of rock above the spring and, after a short distance through fairly steep walls, widened into a V, the walls gradually sinking into the plain. The water itself, after moving along in a slow seep a few hundred feet, disappeared back into the sandy soil. Grass was plentiful, both in the V and on the nearby prairie.

[181]

Twisted Foot took his bow and went out. Well-marked game trails led to the spring from every direction. He soon saw antelope and killed one, just as the sun was rising.

Back at the spring, while a chunk of the antelope was cooking, Twisted Foot considered his situation. This place, with its water and grass, was well-suited to the important purpose he had in mind, but he did not forget the men with white skins. Determined to take no chance that they might surprise him, he kept the horses tied closely in the cover during the next two days and he himself spent the time on the surrounding crests, watching. He saw many creatures of the prairie, antelope, deer, wolves and buffalo, but nothing of men, either white-skinned or red.

Reassured, the young Comanche went about the important matter he had in mind on the morning of the third day. He had determined that when next he went to Kills Something's village, an event he looked forward to eagerly now, he would be on the back of a horse—his horse. He hoped to be riding as securely and gracefully as did the men with the white skins. Not only would he show his people a horse but he would show them that he, the crippled one with the deformed foot, was the master of the horse, able to move with greater speed than any man could run. He would prove to them in a manner they could not doubt that the words of Old Man Crazy had been true. And especially he liked the thought of

Kills Something and One Grass and Follows Bees and the others staring in wide-eyed amazement and admiration when he went galloping among the wickiups. But to achieve this, he knew he had much to learn.

From the antelope hide he made a leather head harness, such as he had seen on the heads of the horses of the men with the white skins, and he took this to Likes-His-Ears-Scratched and put it on his head. It consisted of a loop about the horse's jaw and nose, held in place by a longer loop that went up around the horse's head. Of course he did not have a bit—the hard little stick that went in the horse's mouth—but for the long strings he tied a leather thong to the nose loop, just under the horse's chin. He was not certain just how all this would work, but when he took hold of the thong and turned away Likes-His-Ears-Scratched followed readily. Twisted Foot led him out of the brush.

The horse stood quietly and Twisted Foot remembered that he had been on the animal's back before, but still he was hesitant. It was all so new and strange, and Likes-His-Ears-Scratched was so big and strong. His back bounced up and down so fast when he went. But Twisted Foot knew he had to do it. He gripped the mane in the fingers of one hand and jumped up. He landed awkwardly on the horse's back but, since he had lacked confidence in his jump, was not far enough over and fell back. Likes-His-Ears-Scratched moved a step or two, then halted. "Stop," Twisted Foot said, knowing that he had made a poor attempt. He determined to do better and grasped the horse's mane again. This time he jumped strongly and landed with his stomach across Likes-His-Ears-Scratched's back. He felt a little panic at finding himself there and quickly scrambled about until he was astride the horse. He held tightly to the mane. Likes-His-Ears-Scratched did not move. Twisted Foot relaxed a little and was quite content that the horse was still. He sat up a bit straighter and his confidence increased. It really was not so far to the ground as he had imagined, and he did not feel in any danger of falling. But he did not release his grip on the mane.

After a time, Twisted Foot began to wonder why Likes-His-Ears-Scratched did not go. He had before, and with bewildering speed. Now, however, he just stood. Twisted Foot could not understand it. Was Likes-His-Ears-Scratched waiting for something, and if so—what? "Go," Twisted Foot said, but not very strongly for he did not want the horse to go as swiftly as that other time. Likes-His-Ears-Scratched did not move. "Go," Twisted Foot said again, with more real meaning. Also, he pressed his heels experimentally against the horse's side.

Likes-His-Ears-Scratched took a few steps forward, but then stopped. Twisted Foot wondered why—why had he stopped? Then he noticed that Likes-His-Ears-Scratched was holding his head slightly to one side, as he had when the rope was dragging. Now, however, the rope was not about his neck. Then Twisted Foot realized what it was

—the thong he had tied to the nose loop. He had forgotten to keep it in his hand and it was dragging on the ground. This was the reason Likes-His-Ears-Scratched would not go. He did not want to step on the thong. Twisted Foot was relieved by this explanation of the horse's unexpected behavior, and he knew it was his fault. He should have kept the end of the thong in his hand. He didn't, however, know just what to do about it. Now that he was up, he was reluctant to get off, fearing that getting on the next time would not be so easy.

While Twisted Foot was considering the problem, Likes-His-Ears-Scratched, either purposely or not, made an unexpected move that helped to solve it. The horse saw a tempting tuft of grass and put his head down to eat it. Twisted Foot could not get his fingers out of the tangled mane quickly enough to keep from being pulled over the horse's withers. He knew a quick feeling of panic when he found himself falling, but this did not last long, being ended by a solid thump that knocked the breath out of him. He lay there on his back, staring up at the blue sky and wondering if he would die. But immediately he knew he wasn't hurt, and Likes-His-Ears-Scratched had shied away. He scrambled hastily to his feet and said, "Do not run, Likes-Your-Ears-Scratched. I did not mean to do it." The horse eyed him somewhat dubiously. "Stay still," he went on anxiously. "Stay still until I can get the thong. I did not mean to do it."

Likes-His-Ears-Scratched became calm and presently

Twisted Foot had the thong. Relieved, he leaned against the horse. Then he realized that the dreaded calamity had happened—he had fallen from the horse's back. It had happened, and he was still there, unhurt. Resolutely he turned to the horse again, and this time, while climbing up, he kept the chin thong in his hand. This time, too, he did not lock his fingers so tightly in the long neck hair.

Likes-His-Ears-Scratched started at once and willingly, without waiting for Twisted Foot to say go. He walked over the grass. Gradually Twisted Foot became accustomed to the motion and relaxed. It wasn't difficult, not really. Instead, it was actually pleasant to be up there, riding over the prairie. Twisted Foot began to feel pleased with himself. This was a new life, thrilling and exciting. Never again would he be content to walk. That must have been what Old Man Crazy meant. But how could Old Man Crazy know, never having been on a horse?

More excitement was coming, and before Twisted Foot was ready for it. Likes-His-Ears-Scratched was a wise horse. Walking across the prairie, he soon sensed the lack of guidance and direction in his rider. The hand was slack on the chin thong and there was no decision in the knees. The rider's balance was timid and lagging. Likes-His-Ears-Scratched knew he was in command of the situation, and, being in command, he decided to do what he wanted to, which was to return to the gray mare and the comfortable shade of the trees. He was too wise, however, to make an abrupt turn. Instead he went in a big circle

and presently was headed back to the water hole. Pleased at the success of his strategy and impatient to get the ride over with, he increased his gait to a trot.

Twisted Foot found himself bouncing up and down in a most confusing and uncomfortable manner. He locked both hands in Likes-His-Ears-Scratched's mane and tried to glue himself to the horse, which made the jolting worse. "Stop . . . stooooppp, Likes-Your-Ears-Scratched," he pleaded.

But Likes-His-Ears-Scratched had the cool shade in mind and knew that now was the time to take advantage of the uncertainty on his back. He increased his gait to a long trot, causing Twisted Foot to cling desperately. Likes-His-Ears-Scratched galloped, and presently stretched the gallop to a run.

"Stoopp, stoooppp," Twisted Foot cried unhappily, but his voice had neither emphasis nor confidence.

Likes-His-Ears-Scratched continued to run. He was in fine condition and enjoyed running. And because Twisted Foot's heels were digging unpleasantly into his flanks, he kicked up his heels. That did it for Twisted Foot. He lost his balance, clung for a few seconds by the mane, and then knew it was useless. He saw the ground coming, turned so as to hit on his side, and rolled. He was up almost immediately, not hurt but chagrined and half angry. He had fallen off again. "You . . . you . . ." he cried helplessly at the departing horse. He started to run after the stallion but immediately knew it was hopeless. Likes-

[188]

His-Ears-Scratched galloped on and disappeared into the little canyon, leaving Twisted Foot to walk home from his first ride.

Twisted Foot became concerned as he walked, afraid that Likes-His-Ears-Scratched might disappear, but when he reached the water hole the stallion was standing near the gray mare, already half asleep. He lifted his head and looked at Twisted Foot with great innocence. But Twisted Foot was hot and dirty from his falls and he was not fooled. "You," he said firmly. "You stand still, Likes-Your-Ears-Scratched. I am going to ride you, and you are going to do what I wish and go where I want you to. I am your master."

Recognizing the authority in the voice, the stallion stood perfectly still while Twisted Foot walked up and took the chin thong. Without hesitation Twisted Foot climbed up. "Go," he said, and Likes-His-Ears-Scratched walked obediently from the trees and back to the prairie.

CHAPTER SIXTEEN

AFTER THAT, Twisted Foot never faltered. He quickly gained confidence and worked with the horses, riding and handling them, by the hour. The gray mare, he discovered, had a wonderfully tranquil disposition, being even more gentle and obedient than the stallion. And like the stallion, she was quick and light on her feet, though she lacked his powerful, sweeping stride. Twisted Foot rode her frequently and she soon became an accepted member of the group, second only to Likes-His-Ears-Scratched in importance. Twisted Foot marveled at the turn of events which had enabled him to have two horses instead of one, and now it was not in his mind that she should go back to the possession of the men with white skins.

Quickly, too, Twisted Foot learned the fundamentals of riding. In this, the wise horses were of much help, being willing in obedience and giving him many hints as to the signals and methods used by the men with white skins. He learned how to make them go, and to make them stop. He learned to guide them by pulling on the chin thong in the direction he wished to go. He developed a natural balance that enabled him to ride freely and easily, and soon he learned the importance of balance in control. Through balance, the horses could often determine his desires quicker than he could signal with hand or foot. This was something even Old Man Crazy had not suspected.

The head harness broke one day, and Twisted Foot, not wishing to take time to repair it, tied the end of the leather thong around the horse's lower jaw as a temporary substitute. This worked so well that he never did repair the head harness. He felt the need of a saddle and made one, of bobcat skin, held in place by a strong leather strap that went around the horse's body. He knew nothing of stirrups and made the saddle just a single thickness, for he liked to feel the warm ripple of the horses' backs beneath him as they skimmed over the grass.

The days at this water hole passed, pleasant and rewarding, but Twisted Foot did not forget that all this was only the preparation for another event of great importance. One morning he put his thong bridle and the light bobcat pelt saddle on the silky-coated stallion and turned the horse's head east, toward the country of the stunted juniper and rocky ravines. He did not need to look back to know that the faithful gray mare was following with the pad and bundle cover on her back. Twisted Foot now knew the horses so well, their moods and habits, that he unhesitatingly turned them free in the evenings and mornings to graze, no longer concerned about the possibility of their leaving him. His one worry had been that some roving man, a Ute or, worse, a man with white skin, might see them, and for that reason he never left them alone very long.

This morning he was leaving the spring. He had learned about the horses and trained himself to ride and control them. Now he was ready to return to the village, to show Kills Something, One Grass, and the others the near miracle. He was particularly anxious to see Follows Bees, to watch the expression on his brother's face when Follows Bees saw the horses. Follows Bees would be unable to believe it, but he would teach him to ride and together they would roam wide over the prairies, going to places where none of the Comanches had ever been before and he, not even thinking of his crippled foot, would go as swiftly and as easily as his fleet brother. Now he knew the joy of a free and powerful stride over the grass.

The prairie stretched before them, from a distance appearing flat but being actually a long succession of low rises and wide shallow swales, broken occasionally by dry washes, cut so deceptively in the grass that it required a practiced eye to detect them before reaching almost their very edges. It was a country Twisted Foot knew and loved, a country of warmth and change, of surprise, and the mystery of the great distances. Too, it was a country of plenty, rich in the sources of the most desirable food and shelter.

Likes-His-Ears-Scratched paused at the top of a rise and swiveled his dark ears forward. Twisted Foot followed the horse's gaze and saw the dark objects. "Big humps," he told Likes-His-Ears-Scratched. "Go on." Buffalo were a common sight on the plains.

The stallion moved on obediently, no more concerned than his master. They crossed a wide swale and climbed another rise. At this crest it was Twisted Foot who ordered the halt. "Ho," he said and twitched the jaw thong. The buffalo were much closer and could be seen clearly, dark, high-shouldered figures. They were grazing steadily, massive heads to the soft wind. What attracted Twisted Foot's attention, however, was not the dark figures, but a white one. It was a rare albino, the animal of magic powers with the great spirits. Immediately a wish leaped full-grown into Twisted Foot's mind.

He had seen the men with the white skins run antelope on their horses, and he knew that the antelope were fully as fleet as the buffalo, though not so big and powerful and dangerous. Choicest of all the animals from the standpoint of the Indians, buffalo were also, because of their wariness, speed, and strength, the most difficult to secure.

Could a horse change this? Twisted Foot, who never yet had killed a buffalo, was awed by the thought. It would be too good, too wonderful to be true. But with a swift-running horse like Likes-His-Ears-Scratched . . . Twisted Foot wished he knew whether it had ever been done, even by the men with white skins and their smoke-sticks. Old Man Crazy in all his talk had not mentioned such a thing, but neither had Old Man Crazy mentioned the running of antelope, and he, Twisted Foot, had seen that with his own eyes, had seen the men set off after the animals, and had seen them come back with freshly killed carcasses across their horses in front of them. Still, the buffalo had wicked curved horns and ran with a blind indifference to what was before them. He remembered having once seen the broken, trampled body of a hunter unfortunate enough to have been caught in their path.

But a white buffalo, one of those rare creatures by which the Indian gods set so much store! Indeed, no man of the village, not even Kills Something, had yet killed a white buffalo. Such an opportunity might never come again. A white skin, with the two horses, would unquestionably earn him a high position among his people. Kills Something and the old men would know that his crippled foot was no hindrance to his becoming a leader. Still, would it not be foolish to risk what he had already achieved, his proud horse and even his own life? There would be time later to learn if a horse could be useful in hunting buffalo.

The white buffalo was feeding among the others. None of them was yet aware of Twisted Foot's presence. His eyes searched the country leading to them. There was a swale, a nose which he could pass behind, another swale and a short rise at the top of which, if they continued feeding in their present direction, he should be close to them, not near enough for an arrow but as close as he could hope to get while on the back of a horse. Could Likes-His-Ears-Scratched do it? Could he match strides with the hard-running buffalo and keep his feet over the rough ground? Was he bold enough to drive in close to the pounding feet and dangerous horns?

"Go," Twisted Foot said and guided the stallion into the swale. Likes-His-Ears-Scratched was the finest horse, he was sure, that ever walked the prairies. If they failed, it would be no fault of his.

The gray mare followed and Twisted Foot wished that he might temporarily be rid of her. She could be of no assistance and might be in the way, might even get hurt. But there wasn't a tree in sight or anything to tie her to. Also, he knew that Likes-His-Ears-Scratched might put up a fuss at leaving her behind, might even neigh and startle the buffalo. He would have to let her come.

Despite his impatience, he kept Likes-His-Ears-Scratched at a walk around the point and into the next swale, to save the horse's strength for what was to come. The mare came sleepily behind, all unaware of what was impending. Twisted Foot hoped she would not get ahead and frighten the buffalo before he was ready. Going up the slope, he took the strong bow from his back and his heaviest and sharpest arrow from his quiver, and he held them both in his left hand, meanwhile shortening the jaw thong in his right. This caused Likes-His-Ears-Scratched to raise his head alertly.

Twisted Foot's heart was pounding his ribs excitedly as they topped the rise. There before him were the buffalo, still feeding into the wind. They were not as near as he had hoped, but further stealth was useless. He clapped his heels to Likes-His-Ears-Scratched's flanks and the brown horse leaped forward. In two jumps he was at a run.

An old bull at the edge of the herd swung about, searching with his small, nearsighted eyes. He let out a loud warning snort and the herd was in motion, a sea of bobbing humps, great cloven hooves pounding the sod, short tails waving in frantic flight.

Twisted Foot was afraid the distance was too great, but Likes-His-Ears-Scratched was running with a strong sure stride. Twisted Foot leaned low over the horse's neck and cried, "Go, go!" The answering burst of smooth driving strength beneath him thrilled his whole being. "Go, Likes-Your-Ears-Scratched! Go!"

The brown stallion seemed to know what was wanted of him. He stretched his lean body close to the grass and fairly flew with great ground-eating leaps. Twisted Foot was thankful for all those long hours he had spent learning to ride. His confidence in Likes-His-Ears-Scratched strengthened, but he became less sure of himself. How could he ever draw his bow?

The stallion began to gain on the buffalo, slowly but surely. The distance to the bobbing humps lessened. Dust rolled up and came back, blurring vision. Likes-His-Ears-

Scratched sliced boldly through it, guided by the pound of hooves. Had the quarry been just any buffalo, or even a fat young cow, Twisted Foot soon could have made his try. And he was tempted. There was a strong young bull, certainly a worth-while triumph for a first run, a fine hide to take to his father's lodge. And no one would ever know about the albino.

He looked again for the albino and found it running in the herd, well to the front, in a place so difficult to reach that he became discouraged. It seemed hopeless. But Likes-His-Ears-Scratched, head and neck stretched low and big nostrils flared to the wind, was running stronger than ever, his movements beautifully attuned to the balance of his light brown-skinned rider. Twisted Foot's determination returned. "Go. Go," he cried.

The brown horse gained steadily, moving up along the edge of the running herd. Presently he gained a position well toward the front, boldly near the bobbing humps and horns, their footing indistinct in the dust. Twisted Foot watched for an opening, well knowing the buffalo were half-blinded by this same dust. There was a space, a narrow space, stubby horns behind and waving tails in front. He shifted his weight toward it and the stallion responded gamely. Then they were in, running side by side with the buffalo. There was blowing and pounding behind them and driving, straining backs in front, and dust swirled from the frenzied hooves. Twisted Foot thought of the trampled hunter, then put the thought out of his mind. The hunter had not been on the back of a marvelous horse.

The albino was a dozen humps away. Twisted Foot watched his chance. There was an opening, and another. Now his leg rubbed the thick curly hair of a great bull's shoulder. He beat the animal out of the way with his bow and sent Likes-His-Ears-Scratched into the space. He caught a glimpse of the gray mare, running strongly on the outside of the herd and neighing her excitement, and he had time for a little hope that she wouldn't come into this hectic confusion too.

Now only two animals were between him and the albino. He forged ahead of one, struck it a solid blow across the nose with his bow, and had the satisfaction of seeing it lag behind. The second ran strongly and for a few seconds he could get neither in front of nor behind it. He leaned over and screamed at it and struck it with his bow, but it seemed insensible to everything except the wild panic that was keeping it in flight. Likes-His-Ears-Scratched crowded it, shoulder to shoulder, stride against stride, and finally it swerved, enough to put it behind the albino.

Then at last, Twisted Foot was in position. The stallion was carrying him smoothly and strongly at the side of the white buffalo, and he could see that it was a splendid animal. Now it was up to him. He didn't know how he could take from the strength that was holding him to the horse enough to pull the bow, but he had to. He couldn't fail

Likes-His-Ears-Scratched now. Slackening his grip on the jaw thong, he gave the stallion a completely free head. He gripped with his knees and legs and put his confidence in the horse's strong smooth stride. Please do not swerve or stumble, he thought. His hand shook as he notched the arrow. He drew the string back in a swift movement, back to his very chin. He leaned over until the arrow was pointed directly at the white side and released it. He saw it leap and drive in between the ribs, saw the buffalo recoil from the shock, saw the falter in its stride and knew the shot had been good. He waited no longer but straightened, caught up the jaw thong and began to look for a way out of the mass.

It was nearer to the front than to either of the sides, and there was less dust there too, so he pressed Likes-His-Ears-Scratched forward, between two shaggy backs. The stallion pulled up among the doggedly-pounding leaders. He ran at their sides and past their massive heads. Presently he was in front, out in the clear. Twisted Foot kept him running steadily until they had gained enough to angle to the side. They swept across in front of the first of the low churning heads. Knowing a great thankfulness, Twisted Foot sat up straight and put gentle pressure against the jaw thong. "Stop. Stop, Likes-Your-Ears-Scratched," he said with deep affection, and let the trembling stallion take his own time in coming to a halt.

Likes-His-Ears-Scratched presently turned, his head up, his nostrils red and flaring widely, his lean flanks heaving from the recent exertion. Twisted Foot sat on his back and watched the buffalo gallop madly on into the distance. The gray mare came pounding up, neighing her anxiety and indignation at such a hectic and foolish business.

Twisted Foot looked at her, jerked his head in a gesture of approval, and said, "You did well too, Carries-A-Bundle."

He touched Likes-His-Ears-Scratched with his heels and turned him back along the beaten, scarred swath toward the place where the great shaggy white animal lay motionless. In the future the lodges of Kills Something's village would not want for meat and hides.

But proud as he was of the white buffalo, the young Comanche with the twisted foot was even prouder of his horse.

CHAPTER SEVENTEEN

For strength and bravery, Twisted Foot ate the liver of the white buffalo. He took the skin, to be offered later by the people of his village in a ceremony of respect and reverence to their gods. He handled the skin with due regard for its mystic qualities, and put it across the brown horse in front of him before he rode on.

He halted early that afternoon at a sluggish stream. While the horses grazed, he stretched and scraped the hide, removing all fat and flesh. He left it pegged tight to the ground that night and all the next day for preliminary drying. The following morning, he rolled it carefully with the hair side in before placing it across Likes-His-Ears-Scratched's withers, where he could carry it carefully before him, being unwilling to trust it to the back of the gentle mare. Not in all the time that he could remember had his people been fortunate enough to have a white buffalo skin with which to evoke the blessings of the great spirits, and he knew it would be the beginning of a new period of faith and courage.

Two days of steady riding brought Twisted Foot to the

ravine country, the country of sharp twisting ridges and runs and clumps of stunted evergreen. It was a barren land, dry and flinty, scarce of game, offering little but the security of its innumerable hiding places. It was a land of retreat for those hard pressed by their foes, a place to crouch in fear and lick grievous wounds.

Twisted Foot knew the country well. Of recent years Kills Something's band had spent much time there, hiding from the overpowering Utes. They had ventured to the prairies, to the country of easier living and more abundant game, only to be driven back by the fierce and vigilant war parties of the stronger tribe. Twisted Foot himself had taken part in these humiliating flights.

He rode up among the ridges, searching. The concealment of the country could baffle friends as well as foes, but Twisted Foot knew the trails, the water holes and Kills Something's favorite hiding places. He soon found the ashes of a camp, but they had long been cold. Many weeks, even moons, had passed since Kills Something's return to the area. Twisted Foot went from place to place. He found other camps, ashes, worn out moccasins, hastily built wickiups that had later been abandoned. He found water holes gone dry and gameless canyons. He found a new grave on a hillside and two at the base of a cliff, and he thought of Old Man Crazy in the narrow winding prairie wash.

He searched and searched, even into the great long canyon which twisted far back into the high mesa, a place of such natural defense that not even the bold Utes would dare penetrate it. But Kills Something and his people were nowhere to be found. Twisted Foot became worried. Perhaps the white buffalo robe that he carried across his horse in front of him was not such good fortune after all. He wondered if the gods could be angry with him for having killed it, if they deemed the use of a horse wrong and unfair.

Presently, after days of relentless seeking, Twisted Foot could come to no conclusion save that Kills Something's village was not in the ravine country. It had been there, had traveled the trails and visited the water holes, but now it was gone. Where? He searched diligently for messages that might have been left for him, for piled stones or arranged sticks, for a scrap of buckskin that might contain a picture, but he found nothing. This led him to believe that his people had given up all hope of his returning.

At a favorite water hole, Twisted Foot built a low mound of stones. With a charred stick he drew a picture on the piece of white skin he used for an antelope flag. It was a crude picture, but the animal could not be mistaken for an elk, a deer or a buffalo. And the two-legged figure on this animal's back had a twisted right foot. Twisted Foot knew the picture told a strange and exciting story, but it was a strange and exciting story that he had to tell. He folded the buckskin carefully and placed it under the top stone of the mound. Then he arranged other and smaller stones in the form of an arrow, pointing toward the prairies.

Twisted Foot had decided to return to the plains. Grass was abundant there for his horses, which was important, and food for himself would be easy to secure. Also, now having horses, he had but small concern for the Utes. He knew he could easily outdistance them. He did, however, propose to be vigilant of the men with the white skins, for they were unaccountably hostile and had the long smoke-sticks.

Leaving the ravine country, Twisted Foot moved slowly back into the prairie, keeping a close watch on all sides and remembering that he himself, because of the horses, could be seen from long distances. He came to a clean stream where there was an abundance of grass and some tree cover, and he remained here three days, letting his horses graze their fill, and securing a fat young antelope for his own food. He found time here, also, to continue the process of softening and curing the white buffalo hide.

Leaving this stream early one bright morning, Twisted Foot had not ridden far before he discovered a dust cloud on the horizon. Immediately he thought of the men with the white skins and had an impulse to ride in the opposite direction. He watched the cloud for several minutes and determined that it was moving, but not very rapidly. There was the possibility, of course, that it might be buffalo, trailing across the dry dusty plain. Antelope would lift dust too, but only if they were traveling faster than that.

Twisted Foot decided that he would not run until he knew what he was running from, and if the men with the white skins were in this section of the prairies it would be well for him to know it. He turned Likes-His-Ears-Scratched's head in the direction of the dust. At each rise, Twisted Foot halted for a new survey. He found that while the cloud seemed nearer, he could make out nothing at its base. He went on, becoming more and more cautious, and as he drew nearer, the cloud was apparently traveling faster. Soon he could see that whatever was raising it was traveling through a nearby swale. He dismounted, tied leather strings around his horses' noses to keep them from nickering and led them forward. One careful glance over the rise and his eyes widened in surprise.

It was not buffalo or the men with the white skins. It was Indians. He saw their black hair, their dark, skin-clad bodies. They were moving through the swale, women and children with bundles on their backs, dogs dragging heavily-laden travois, the ends of which were raising most of the dust. And there was something about the movement which arrested Twisted Foot's attention, something hurried and furtive. Where, too, were the men and older boys?

Twisted Foot was pondering this when, through the curtain of dust behind, he caught a glimpse . . . a kneeling form, a deep-drawn bow, a brandished war club. There was fighting! A battle was going on! Twisted Foot turned his attention back to the women and children, and he recognized them. There was Tule Woman, his own mother, and Rabbit Woman, his mother's sister, and Kills Something's heavy-bodied squaw. It was Kills Something's village. It was his own people.

Quickly, Twisted Foot realized what had happened. Hungry for antelope meat and hoping for buffalo hides, Kills Something, after a period of hiding in the ravines, had decided to return to the plains and, as had happened before, the Utes had discovered the village. But this time there had not been sufficient warning and the Utes were close behind. Kills Something and his men were fighting at the rear while the women and children were seeking to escape.

Twisted Foot's first impulse was to hasten down the slope and give his assistance. Then he thought about his horses and was reluctant to leave them. The stallion had his head up and his ears tilted forward, listening to the sounds of the battle. Twisted Foot knew he could leave the gray mare, but not Likes-His-Ears-Scratched. Too much could happen. Then he remembered—remembered that the Utes were afraid of horses, that they believed horses were the embodiment of the evil spirits. He turned and threw himself up on the stallion's back. He let out a wild, piercing yell—hoping the Utes still believed it.

As he sped through the dust curtain, he felt the white buffalo skin slip to one side and he grabbed the edge of it with his free hand. He yelled in the dust and burst through beyond it, with the skin floating behind him like a great white flag, adding both height and size to the horse. With both hands busy, Twisted Foot was unable to use his bow, but this did not daunt him. He gave a screaming yell and headed his horse straight at the Indians, savagely determined to run them down. And the stallion, trained in obedience, answered boldly. He charged full tilt into the melee, knocking both Comanches and Utes right and left. And the gray mare, with neither rope nor rider, came snorting and plunging behind him, bowling over those just picking themselves up, and sending others scurrying.

Twisted Foot whirled the white buffalo skin above his head and screamed, "Kill the Utes! Kill the Utes!" The stallion whirled back and came in from another angle, his eyes blazing, his powerful teeth bared and the interior of his nostrils as red as blood. "Kill the Utes!" Twisted Foot yelled again, as much to tell Kill Something's people that he was a friend as to terrorize the enemy. "Kill the Utes!" The wind caught the white skin and whipped it about his body. The gray mare's shoulder caught a tall warrior solidly and sent him spinning. Another sought to dodge from the stallion's hoofs, but was not quick enough. "Kill the Utes!"

The Utes could stand no more. They broke and fled,

racing frantically over the grass. Twisted Foot charged behind them, thundering at their heels, bowling over two laggards for good measure. He beat at their fleeing backs with the white skin. "Eat the Utes! Eat the Utes!" he cried, as if giving directions to an evil spirit that galloped and turned and whirled beneath him. In their panic, the Utes left the ground littered with bows and lances and war clubs. They threw themselves to the ground, as if expecting to be stricken, then jumped up and ran again.

Twisted Foot was too wise, however, to press his good luck too far. Presently he whirled his horse and went galloping back to Kills Something's men, who were huddled in a tight, wide-eyed group, only slightly less frightened than the Utes. "You have nothing to fear," he called to them, halting the horse.

No one spoke for several seconds, then Kills Something asked humbly, "Who comes to help the Comanches?"

"Do you not know me?" Twisted Foot cried in quick surprise. "I am Twisted Foot."

"Twisted Foot?"

"Twisted Foot? Can it be?"

"It is! It is Twisted Foot," Follows Bees, himself now with a man's full growth, cried happily. "He still lives after all."

"Yes," Twisted Foot said, his manner touched with pride.

But Kills Something and his men were looking at the two horses. "What is this strange creature that strikes

thunder from the earth and carries you so swiftly and so well?" Kills Something asked presently, wonder and uncertainty in his voice.

"It is a horse," Twisted Foot told them.

"A horse?" Kills Something repeated, with a confused shake of his head. "What is a horse? Is it a spirit, brother?"

Twisted Foot thrilled at the use of this term of respect from his chief, and it reminded him of another older man for whom he now had a great regard. "Yes," he said, "it is a spirit—it is the spirit of Old Man Crazy. Old Man Crazy will come among us no more. But remember him, my people, for he has put wings on our feet and great strength in our hands."

They stared at him, not yet comprehending. The women, who had been ahead, began drifting curiously back to the group.

Twisted Foot gave the buffalo skin a quick fling and sent it whirling down before them. "Look!" he cried. "The skin of a great white buffalo! The favor of the gods will be ours. Old Man Crazy's words were true. The Comanches will rule the plains."

From his superior height, he looked at them proudly, well knowing that it was the beginning of a new era. The Indian's saddle was up.